STEVIE TAKES A SPILL

"Thank God you had on a hard hat," said Carole.

"I think I should call a doctor," Deborah said.

"No, I'm okay, really," Stevie said, pushing herself to a sitting position.

"Here, I'll help you up," Lisa offered. Stevie took her hand. She stood up carefully.

"Boy, I can't believe Veronica would be so incredibly stupid as to cause an accident like this!" Lisa snapped. "Every time I think she's reached the limit, she finds another limit to reach!"

A genuine look of puzzlement crossed Stevie's face. "Veronica? What's she got to do with this? How could a nice girl like Veronica cause something like this to happen?"

Lisa and Carole looked at one another.

"Call a doctor," said Lisa.

"No, call an ambulance," said Carole.

THE SADDLE CLUB
SUPER #4

DREAM HORSE

BONNIE BRYANT

A SKYLARK BOOK
NEW YORK · TORONTO · LONDON · SYDNEY · AUCKLAND

I would like to express my special thanks to Marion Barritt, whose personal experience suggested this story, and to Michael Bird, to whom I am indebted for the technical accuracy about soaring. I get credit for any errors on that subject—or any other.

BB

RL 5, 009–012

DREAM HORSE

A Bantam Skylark Book / July 1996

Skylark Books is a registered trademark of Bantam Books, a division of Bantam Doubleday Dell Publishing Group, Inc. Registered in U.S. Patent and Trademark Office and elsewhere.

"The Saddle Club" is a registered trademark of Bonnie Bryant Hiller. The Saddle Club design/logo, which consists of a riding crop and a riding hat, is a trademark of Bantam Books.

"USPC" and "Pony Club" are registered trademarks of The United States Pony Clubs, Inc., at The Kentucky Horse Park, 4071 Iron Works Pike, Lexington, KY 40511-8462.

ISBN 0-553-48367-6

Published simultaneously in the United States and Canada.

Bantam Books are published by Bantam Books, a division of Bantam Doubleday Dell Publishing Group, Inc. Its trademark, consisting of the words "Bantam Books" and the portrayal of a rooster, is Registered in U.S. Patent and Trademark Office and in other countries. Marca Registrada. Bantam Books, 1540 Broadway, New York, New York 10036.

PRINTED IN THE UNITED STATES OF AMERICA

OPM   0 9 8 7 6 5 4 3 2 1

For Michael

1

STEVIE LAKE FOCUSED all of her concentration on the jump in front of her. She could feel the power of her horse, and she could see the brown earth beneath her horse's hooves. She could sense the warm summer sun on her back. But the only thing she knew was the jump itself.

"Come on, Belle," she whispered to her horse. "You can do it."

She leaned forward in the saddle, rose ever so slightly, and gave Belle some rein. The horse moved her head forward, anticipating the jump. Then the mare's powerful rear legs propelled horse and rider up and over. For a moment Stevie felt as if she and Belle were one being, soaring in unison. A split second later Belle's forelegs met the ground and found footing, carrying the rest of her body forward until her hindquarters landed. It was smooth and easy.

"Like the wind!" Stevie declared joyously.

"Great job!" Lisa Atwood called as she clapped for her friend. Lisa was sitting on the fence of the schooling ring.

"You've got to remember to hold your hands still," said Carole Hanson. Carole was sitting next to Lisa on the fence, watching carefully so she could critique everything.

Carole, Stevie, and Lisa were best friends. They sometimes laughed about it, because often it seemed to them that they couldn't have been more different. But they had one thing in common that was more important than all of their differences: They loved horses. They loved everything that had to do with horses. They loved to ride them, and they also loved taking care of them, feeding them, grooming them—even mucking out their stalls. They rode together at Pine Hollow Stables. Their instructor, Maximilian Regnery III, and his mother, Mrs. Reg, owned the stable. They kept costs low by asking their riders to help with the chores. Stevie, Carole, and

Lisa pitched in gladly whenever they had the time, and sometimes when they didn't. Taking care of horses and helping friends never seemed like work to the three girls. It usually seemed more like fun.

The girls were so horse-crazy that they'd formed The Saddle Club. It was a simple club. It had only two rules. Members had to be horse-crazy, and they had to be willing to help one another out, whether they knew they needed help or not.

Twelve-year-old Carole was the most experienced rider of the three girls. She sometimes said she'd been born to ride. Carole had been around horses since she was a very little girl. She knew exactly what she wanted to do when she grew up, too. She was going to be a competitive rider. Or maybe she was going to be a trainer. Sometimes it seemed that being a breeder would be the best. Or perhaps a vet. Then again, maybe she'd be all those things!

When it came to horses, Carole was all business. She never forgot anything that had to do with the welfare of a horse, particularly of her own beloved bay gelding, Starlight. When it came to anything but horses, Carole could be rather forgetful. Her father, a colonel in the Marine Corps, often said that she'd leave her head at home if it weren't attached so securely.

"That's silly, Dad," Carole said. "The reason I don't leave my head at home is because I'm going to need it when I get to the stable!"

Her friends suspected she wasn't entirely joking.

Lisa, who was thirteen, never forgot anything. She was always organized and logical. Her clothes never got wrinkled. Her homework was never late. She was a straight-A student, a teacher's dream. She was the newest rider of the three girls, but she worked so hard at it— as at everything she did—that she was almost as good as her friends. Max said she was one of the fastest learners he'd ever taught. Lisa was good at other things, too. She'd taken music lessons, ballet lessons, and painting lessons. She liked to act and sing and had even starred in a local production of *Annie*. Although there were many things she enjoyed doing, she liked riding horses most of all.

Stevie was as mischievous as Lisa was organized. The twelve-year-old often joked that she spent about half her time in hot water. Her friends pointed out to her that she spent the other half getting out of hot water, and since they were bound to help her by the rules of The Saddle Club, that meant they had to help with frequent rescue missions. Stevie thought that today was an exception to that. She was working very hard on her jumping skills. Lisa, the totally logical member of the trio, dis-

4

agreed with that. In her opinion, what Stevie was doing by working on her jumps was attempting to get out of hot water. Stevie had made a bet with her boyfriend, Phil Marsten, that she and her horse, Belle, were better jumpers than Phil and his horse, Teddy. Today's practice was an attempt to help Stevie through her latest "hare-brained notion," as Carole sometimes called them, because Phil had described Belle as a "pretty good jumper." "Pretty good" wasn't anywhere near what Stevie thought of Belle's abilities. *Fabulous* was the word she would have used.

"All right, I'll try again," Stevie said. "And this time, I'll hold my hands still. I've got to get it right because there isn't much time until the contest." She circled Belle around the ring and prepared for another go at the jump.

"Just five more days of this," Lisa remarked to Carole. The jump-off between Stevie and Phil was scheduled for the following Saturday morning before their regular Pony Club meeting. Stevie had wanted it to be in the afternoon on the theory that Belle probably liked sleeping in on Saturday mornings as much as Stevie did, but Phil couldn't do it in the afternoon. His uncle Michael had invited him to fly in his glider with him.

"Imagine thinking that going up in a glider is going to be more important than comparing our horses' jumping.

Why couldn't he fly in the morning?" Stevie had asked indignantly.

"Because gliders require thermals for lift, and it's hard to find thermals before the afternoon sun has warmed the air," Lisa had explained.

"Whatever," Stevie had said.

"How do you know these things?" Carole had asked Lisa.

"I looked it up," Lisa had told her. Carole had thought that was probably why Lisa was a straight-A student.

Stevie circled Belle around the ring and approached the jump again. She often said riding was easy as long as you could remember a million things at the same time: heels down, toes in, back straight, arms relaxed, hands still, weight evenly balanced—and that was just for starters.

Something flashed in her right eye. Someone was walking out of the stable and into the ring.

Stevie turned to look. The minute she turned her head, it changed her balance, and as soon as that happened, Belle hesitated. That meant that Stevie and Belle were too close to the jump when Belle took off. The horse popped the jump and then had to scramble to keep her footing when she landed.

"Ugh!" said Stevie.

"Not pretty," Lisa said.

"The worst!" Carole told her.

"That's a fine way to greet me," said Veronica di-Angelo. The three girls looked at the new arrival. If there were two things The Saddle Club always agreed about, the first was that they were crazy about horses and the second was that Veronica diAngelo was the most obnoxious girl in the entire town of Willow Creek, Virginia—perhaps in the entire world. Veronica was in their Pony Club and took lessons with them. She had her own horse, a very valuable Thoroughbred named Danny. Everything about Veronica, it seemed, was very valuable. Her clothes were from the most exclusive shops at the mall, her hair and nails were always perfect, and she often showed up at Pine Hollow in the backseat of her father's limousine or the front seat of her mother's Mercedes.

"Everything about her is valuable except her personality," Stevie had once remarked. "I wouldn't give you a nickel for that."

Veronica was snobbish, petty, and manipulative. She was pretty and vain and thrived on admiration. She never considered anybody else's feelings, either. It was typical that she'd barged in without considering that her presence might distract Stevie and her horse.

Lisa glanced at Veronica. The other girl was fiddling

7

with an expensive-looking camera. Lisa had taken a number of photography classes at school. Some of her pictures had even been published in the local newspaper. She knew a lot about photography, and she'd never known that Veronica had the slightest interest in it.

Stevie drew Belle to a halt. She was annoyed with herself because she'd allowed Veronica to distract her. She didn't want to give Veronica the satisfaction of knowing that. She put one hand on her hip and looked at the interloper.

"What are you doing with the camera?" she asked. It was a simple question, but Veronica took it as a challenge.

"This isn't just any camera," Veronica said with a sniff. "It's a highly technical piece of photographic equipment. It automatically adjusts itself to the perfect lens opening and focal distance to maximize results."

"Ah, so you can read, too," Stevie said. "I bet that's just what it says in the brochure. Now, tell me, what is it you're planning to maximize results on?"

Lisa and Carole snickered. Stevie was as good at getting under Veronica's skin as Veronica was at getting under Stevie's.

"Actually, I intend to maximize results all the way to Rome, Italy. Perhaps you haven't read about the photographic contest that the mall photography shop, Photo

8

World, is running. First prize for the junior winner is a two-week trip to Rome. I'm already picking out my wardrobe. I think I'll take the—"

"Gee, can I help you with this?" Stevie asked, suddenly eager. "It would be great to have you out of here for two whole weeks! Look, I'll pose for you. I'll be a model. Anything to be sure that you maximize your results."

"Don't bother," said Veronica. "In the first place, I don't need your help. In the second place, the contest rules require that the picture be of somebody doing something that requires skill. You looking like a dummy doesn't take any skill."

Lisa and Carole cringed. Stevie's remark had been mean but mildly funny. Veronica's was simply cruel. If Stevie felt challenged to get even with her, it was likely to be big trouble. Carole was about to suggest that Stevie get back to her jump practice, but Stevie turned Belle and trotted off without the suggestion. There were times when all three of them knew that the only way to deal with Veronica was to ignore her totally.

Stevie circled the ring again and this time kept her focus on the jump. She didn't notice Veronica walking away. She didn't even see her friends perched on the fence. All she saw was the jump, and the only thing on her mind was getting over it in perfect form.

9

"Great!" Lisa said when Belle landed smoothly.

"You're getting it," Carole agreed.

Stevie grinned and rode over to the fence to talk with Lisa and Carole.

"Your hands were much better this time," Carole said. "And it sure makes a difference when you look straight ahead. Now, I think it'll help if you try to remember to keep the lower half of your arm in a straight line with the reins. In other words, no bends from your elbow to the horse's mouth—"

"What's up, girls?" The three girls looked over and saw Deborah Hale Regnery. Deborah was Max's wife, and they liked her very much, though sometimes they wondered how Max could love somebody who knew so little about horses. Deborah was an investigative reporter for a big daily newspaper in Washington, D.C. She and Max had met while she was doing a story on horse stables near the city, and it was love at first sight. In spite of some "help" from The Saddle Club, Deborah and Max had managed to get engaged and married. Now Deborah was learning as much about horses as she could.

"Hi, Deborah," they greeted her.

"Come to watch some fine jumping?" Stevie teased.

"Partly," Deborah said. "I saw the three of you out here, and I thought it was a chance to ask you some questions."

"Sure," said Carole. "What can we do for you?"

"Well, my editor got a tip that there's a shady horse dealer in Rock Ridge—you know where that is?"

"It's west of here," Stevie said. "Near the mountains, right?"

"That's it. The town is named after the craggy mountain ridge that seems to hang over the area," said Deborah. "Anyway, a man named Mickey Denver has been selling horses for years, and he seems to have built up a reputation for less-than-honest dealings."

"That makes me furious," said Carole. "A few bad apples and everybody thinks all horse traders are crooks."

"Like used-car dealers," Lisa suggested.

"Exactly," said Deborah. "The world is full of honest people, but, as Carole said, a few dishonest ones can ruin it for everybody."

"So, what does your editor want you to do?" Stevie asked.

"He wants me to find out if it's true that the man's a crook," said Deborah. "But the trouble is, I don't know any more about buying horses than I do about riding them."

"Well, you're learning how to ride them," Lisa reminded her.

"That's what I mean," Deborah said. "Yesterday when

Max was working with me, he pointed out six things I was doing wrong all at once."

"Only six?" Lisa asked. "My record was eight."

Deborah laughed. "And he keeps telling me what a fast learner you are! Anyway, my editor wants me to go buy a horse from this man. But I really don't know what to look for, and I know if I ask Max, he'll tell me a zillion things and I'll never remember them all. How do you know if you're being bamboozled? I mean, Carole and Stevie, you both have your own horses. What told you these were the right ones for you?"

"Easy," Stevie said. "Love at first sight."

"Ditto," said Carole.

"That isn't helpful," Lisa told her friends. "You two love *any* horse at first sight."

"True," Stevie confessed. "But I was right about Belle, wasn't I?" And then, to prove her point, she turned Belle around with a flourish and began cantering toward the jump.

Everything felt right this time. Stevie kept a straight line from her elbow to Belle's mouth and sank her weight into her heels. She'd show Deborah exactly how it was done. The jump was near. Stevie rose in the saddle, leaning forward and giving Belle some rein. In a split second, she'd signal the horse to jump.

"Yoo-hoo! Stevie! Look at me!"

On the other side of the jump, right outside the ring, stood Veronica, expensive camera to her eye. She waved, calling Stevie's attention.

Stevie's head snapped up. Her balance became skewed. There was a flash. Belle shied. Her hindquarters stopped. Her forelegs flailed wildly. Stevie, totally unprepared for the sudden halt, flew off, soaring gracefully over the jump while Belle remained on the other side. Then there was silence.

Carole gasped. Lisa screamed. They both jumped off the fence. Deborah ran toward Stevie. In a second, Carole had Belle's reins. Lisa and Deborah knelt over Stevie.

Their friend lay motionless on her back with her eyes closed, arms and legs splayed.

"Stevie!" Lisa called.

"Is she okay?" Carole asked, leading Belle over.

Deborah held Stevie's hand and felt her wrist for a pulse. The girls watched in horrified silence. Deborah nodded. She could feel the pulse. But so much else could be wrong!

The moment felt like an eternity. Then Stevie's eyes fluttered open. Deborah made her lie still and asked Stevie to move her arms, legs, hands, and feet one by one. She seemed okay.

Lisa and Carole breathed a sigh of relief.

13

"Thank God you had on a hard hat," said Carole.

"I think I should call a doctor," Deborah said.

"No, I'm okay, really," Stevie said, pushing herself to a sitting position.

"Here, I'll help you up," Lisa offered. Stevie took her hand.

"Boy, I can't believe Veronica would be so incredibly stupid as to cause an accident like this!" Lisa snapped. "Every time I think she's reached the limit, she finds another limit to reach!"

A genuine look of puzzlement crossed Stevie's face. "Veronica? What's she got to do with this? How could a nice girl like Veronica cause something like this to happen?"

Lisa and Carole looked at one another.

"Call a doctor," said Lisa.

"No, call an ambulance," said Carole.

"I already did," said Deborah, tucking her cellular telephone back into her pocket.

"LOOK, HERE IT IS," Lisa said, flipping open her mother's family medical encyclopedia. *Concussion.* That was the word the emergency medical technicians had used as they'd put Stevie into the ambulance at Pine Hollow.

Deborah had been allowed to ride with Stevie to the hospital. Lisa and Carole had to stay behind. They'd used the time well. First, they'd untacked Belle, groomed her, and put her back in her stall. Then they'd hurried over to Lisa's house, where they knew they would get word on their friend. Waiting for phone calls was hard. Lisa had suggested doing some research. "Not that we

15

don't trust the doctors," she had said. "But we know Stevie better than they do."

Carole had agreed. It had only taken them a few minutes to locate the encyclopedia and look up *concussion*.

"It says here a concussion results from impact to the head," Lisa read, her finger running down the column of fine print.

"Check," Carole said. "She definitely had an impact to her head."

"There's usually a headache," Lisa read.

"Check," said Carole, recalling how Stevie's hand had flown up to massage her sore head when she awoke.

"And sometimes loss of consciousness and memory," Lisa concluded.

"Double check," said Carole. "I can't believe she didn't remember Veronica's part in the accident."

"Even if she didn't remember it, how weird was it that she called Veronica 'a nice girl'? I mean, that isn't memory loss—it's a change of personality!"

"Does it say anything about that?" Carole asked.

Lisa finished scanning the entry in the encyclopedia. "Not a word," she said. She closed the book and was returning it to the bookshelf when the phone rang.

Carole answered it. "It's Chad," she said to Lisa. Chad was Stevie's older brother. Carole turned her attention back to the phone. "It's definitely a concussion," Carole reported. "Doctor says it isn't too serious. She'll stay overnight in the hospital to be on the safe side."

"Can we visit?" Lisa asked. Carole relayed the question.

"Sure," Chad said. "But the doctor doesn't want anyone to stay too long. She's supposed to get rest."

"Okay," Carole agreed. "That makes sense. Is there anything she needs, anything we can do for her?"

"As a matter of fact, there is," Chad said. "She wanted me to ask you to call Phil and let him know. I told her I'd be glad to call him. For some reason, I don't think she trusted me to do it."

"Do you think that might have something to do with the time you told Phil the family couldn't wait until the two of them got married so you could have Stevie's room?" Carole asked.

"It was just a suggestion," Chad protested.

"As I recall, Stevie didn't think it showed good judgment," Carole reminded him. Stevie's actual reaction had been somewhat stronger than that. She'd talked seriously to her parents about putting Chad up for adoption.

"Yeah, right. But anyway, can you guys call Phil?"

17

"Glad to," said Carole. "And thanks for letting us know she's okay."

A few minutes later, Lisa had Phil on the telephone and told him what had happened.

"I'll get to the hospital in about an hour," he said, after asking his mother if she could drive him. "I'll meet you there, in front of the place, okay?"

"Well, sure, but is this a good time for you to go over?" Lisa asked.

"Absolutely," said Phil. "I've been working with Teddy, and he's in a foul mood. To tell you the truth, I'm glad for an excuse to stop and give us both a rest. It's almost like what happened to Stevie, in fact. I was out on the jump course, and one of my sister's cats ran out in front of Teddy and spooked him. He shied sideways, and I just flew off him. I landed on my rear with my feet sticking straight out in front of me. I felt so dumb! So, Teddy's spooked, and I'm sore on my saddle seat. Too bad I can't stand up in the car on the way to the hospital! Anyway, I'll see you there in one hour. Bye."

"Bye," Lisa said. She hung up the phone. One hour would give Carole and Lisa just enough time to put together a goody basket for Stevie. There was work to do.

An hour later, Lisa's mother dropped the girls off in front of the hospital at almost exactly the same moment that Mrs. Marsten let Phil out of their car. Lisa was carrying a bag for Stevie. Phil had a bag in his hand, too.

"What did you bring her?" Lisa asked.

"Oh, it's just funny stuff," said Phil, almost embarrassed. "You know, Stevie-like things."

"We know," said Carole. "We brought her a jar of monster goo."

"You're kidding! So did I," said Phil.

"I guess we all know Stevie, huh?" Lisa joked. "Well, we also brought her a book of knock-knock jokes—she'll really like those, don't you think?"

"I hope she likes the book of knock-knock jokes you brought as much as she likes the one I brought," said Phil.

"Really?" asked Carole.

"Really," said Phil. "Like you said, we know Stevie."

The three of them laughed. It turned out that they had brought some different things, too. Phil had a teddy bear—a gift from his horse, he said. Carole and Lisa had brought a Slinky and a selection of cassettes. They were glad to see that Phil was lending her his portable tape player.

The three of them entered the hospital and followed the guard's instructions to find Stevie's room.

Stevie was asleep when the three friends walked in.

19

There was a bandage around her head, secured under her chin. She looked weak and small in the large hospital bed, surrounded by control devices. It looked very official. On closer examination, Lisa realized that one device was to adjust the bed, another was for the television, and the third was to call a nurse. Stevie, always interested in controlling things, was clutching all three in her hands.

Their tiptoe steps awoke Stevie. Her eyes fluttered open. She smiled at her friends.

"How are you feeling?" Phil asked.

"I feel great," Stevie told him. Lisa and Phil each handed her a bag of goodies. Stevie loved her presents and gave her friends hugs. She said there was a young doctor who was going to particularly appreciate what she had in mind for the monster goo.

"What's the bandage for? Did you cut yourself or something?" Carole asked. She couldn't remember anything about the accident that would have required a bandage.

"It's to hold an ice pack in place," Stevie explained. "The thing about concussions is that they come with major headaches. The ice helps. The bandage is just to get sympathy because the doctor says I'm really not very sick."

"Well, that's good news," said Phil. "How can anyone

have any fun in a hospital if they're really sick?" he joked.

Stevie smiled. "Well, if you're really sick, then you won't notice how awful the food is."

"Stevie, you haven't been here long enough to have a meal," Lisa reminded her.

"Oh, right," said Stevie. "But when it comes, I know it'll be awful. All I've had time to do is sleep, and every time I do that, somebody comes in here and asks me what my name is or if I can remember how to count backward from a hundred. Or worse, they want to make sure I'm resting. I haven't even had time for a decent dream."

"Have you had any dreams?" Lisa asked. She always thought dreams were interesting.

"Um, yeah," Stevie said. "An hour and a half ago a nurse woke me up in the middle of a dream about a horse."

"See, she's right. She's not really sick. Dreaming about horses is perfectly normal," said Carole.

"Well, this wasn't so normal," Stevie said. "It was this beautiful bay gelding. He was cantering. He had a gorgeous gait—smooth as could be. Anyway, suddenly something startled the horse, and it got spooked and shied sideways. Next thing I saw was something flying over the horse's head. I don't know what it was, but it

21

was big. Then a nurse came in and asked me who the first president of the United States was. I told her it was Frank Sinatra. That got her to leave pretty fast."

Carole, Lisa, and Phil all laughed. It was just like Stevie to tease a nurse.

The door to Stevie's room opened, and a young doctor came in, accompanied by a nurse with a worried look on her face. Stevie's friends offered to leave, but the doctor said that wouldn't be necessary.

He looked in Stevie's eyes with a penlight and had her follow his finger as he moved it around in front of her.

"Everything seems okay," he said to the nurse. Then he turned back to Stevie. "Um, Stephanie," he said, checking her chart, "do you happen to remember—now, don't worry if everything isn't totally clear to you—but would it be possible for you to recall who the first president of the United States was?"

"Napoléon Bonaparte," she said, without batting an eye.

"Right," said the young doctor, making a mark on her chart. "Thank you." He smiled insincerely and then turned to Lisa, Carole, and Phil. "I think Stephanie could use a little more rest now," he said. "Perhaps you'd like to come back tomorrow?"

Carole was about to set the doctor straight and explain that Stevie was just being funny, but Phil tugged at her sleeve.

"Sure thing, Doctor," he said. "Bye, Stevie. We'll check in tomorrow to see how you're doing."

"I'll be home by tomorrow," she said brightly.

"We'll see," said the doctor.

"Come on," said Phil to Lisa and Carole.

As they scurried through the shiny hallways of the hospital, Lisa asked Phil why he'd been in such a hurry to get out of there.

"Because something very strange is going on," he said.

"Wait a minute. You know she was joking about the president. It's a dumb question. She was just giving a dumb answer," Lisa said.

"Not that. Of course she was teasing. No. It was about the horse in her dream."

"What about it?" asked Carole. "I've seen lots of horses shy. That didn't seem strange to me."

"What was strange was that she was describing exactly what Teddy did at exactly the time she was dreaming about a bay gelding getting spooked. Don't you see? She described what happened to me. And the thing she saw flying over Teddy's head was my body!"

Lisa stopped walking and put her hands on her hips. "Are you telling us you think Stevie's suddenly developed ESP from a bang on her head?" she asked. "Also, keep in mind that the accident that put Stevie here in the hospital is a lot like the one that made you fly over Teddy's head and land on your backside. She was probably just dreaming about her own accident."

Phil paused for a moment. Then he shrugged. "I guess my notion is pretty kooky, isn't it?"

"That's one way to put it," Lisa said.

"I don't know," he said. "But it did seem strange. I mean, it happened to me about an hour and a half ago, and that's when she was having the dream."

"And the same thing happened to her about *three* hours ago," Lisa reminded him. "It makes sense that she would dream about the accident that landed her in the hospital even if her accident involved a mare and her dream was about a gelding."

"I guess," Phil said.

They started walking again and got to the front door of the hospital just as Mrs. Marsten arrived to pick Phil up. Mrs. Marsten offered the girls a lift, but they just had a short walk. They were going over to Pine Hollow on their way back to Lisa's. They all agreed to visit Stevie together the next day. Then Phil drove off with his mother.

"Can you believe that?" Lisa asked. "ESP? Sometimes I wonder who's weirder: Phil or Stevie."

"You know, I feel a little bit sorry for the doctor who

is worrying about whether Stevie—um, I mean *Stephanie*—knows who the first president was."

"Especially if he's the same doctor she was talking about when she mentioned the monster goo," said Lisa.

"The problem with Stevie is that only her best friends understand that what's normal for her may not be exactly what the medical textbooks say is normal for other people."

"And I guess that's why we care about her so much," said Lisa.

3

MAX AND DEBORAH were having a serious conversation when Lisa and Carole arrived. The girls weren't trying to overhear, but it was hard not to because the couple was standing right by Starlight's stall.

"But how are you going to know?" Max asked.

"I don't know, but I will," Deborah said.

"No way. I'm coming."

"You can't," she said. "He'll know who you are. You'll blow my cover! This is my job!"

"It won't make any difference if you don't know what you're writing about," said Max.

"But Max—"

Max spotted Lisa and Carole. "How's Stevie?" he asked. The girls told him about their visit. "When she starts thinking about monster goo and a doctor, you can tell she's on the mend," he said, looking relieved.

"The trouble is that Stevie is so, um . . ." Carole searched for a word.

"Stevian," Lisa supplied.

"Yes, I think you mean *one of a kind*," Deborah translated.

"Right," Carole agreed. "She's so *unique*, it's going to be hard for her doctors to know whether she's thinking straight. I mean, she really got a nurse upset when she told her that Frank Sinatra was the first president of the United States."

Max grinned. "It's nice to know that Stevie is being a challenge for someone else for once!"

Deborah wrinkled her forehead in thought.

"What's up?" Lisa asked her.

"Well, Stevie has a way of solving problems that I sometimes admire. I was just trying to think what she'd do with the problem I have about this investigation into Mickey Denver's business."

"Easy," Lisa said. "She'd tell you to take her along, say she's your daughter, and pretend that you're buying a

27

horse for her. She doesn't know as much as Max, but she knows enough to know when a horse dealer's out-and-out lying."

"Too bad she's in the hospital," Deborah said.

"Ah, but you've got the second- and third-best thing here," said Carole. "Lisa and I can help."

"Great idea," Deborah said brightly. "It's perfect, in fact!"

"Oh, no way!" Max began. "This man is a—"

"Horse trader," said Carole. "We know quite a bit about horses. We'll know if he's trying to pass off a nag as a Thoroughbred."

"He'll see right through you!" Max said sternly.

"Max! Don't forget who had the starring role in *Annie*," Lisa reminded him.

"Right, so you're going to sing to him?" Max asked sarcastically.

Deborah spoke calmly. "Darling," she said, "this is exactly what I need. For one thing, the girls *do* know about horses. For another, a little girl and her doting mother are going to seem like easy marks to a crooked horse trader. It's perfect."

Max seemed to want to say something more. Then he sighed and relented. "I thought life would be simpler with Stevie in the hospital, but it seems that she's here even when she isn't."

"That's the magic of Stevie, isn't it?" Carole asked.

It only took Lisa, Carole, and Deborah a few minutes to set up what Carole called their sting operation. Deborah would be the mother, of course. Lisa would pose as her daughter, and Carole as her daughter's best friend.

"I'm not going to have any trouble playing that part," Carole said.

"I won't have any trouble being a horse-crazy girl," said Lisa. "The hardest part is going to be pretending we don't know much about horses."

"You're right about that," Carole agreed. "Do you think I've got time for a few acting lessons before we go?" she joked.

"Don't worry, dear," said Deborah in a very motherly voice. "If you make any mistakes, I'll see that you're grounded."

Carole snapped a clean salute. "No mistakes, ma'am," she promised.

"It's really not going to be too hard," said Deborah. "Your job is to be totally enthusiastic about any horse he tries to sell us, okay?"

"Deal," Lisa and Carole said.

"Come on, let's call and see when we can meet him," she said.

It only took a few minutes. Mr. Denver seemed pleased to know he had a potential customer. He suggested that they come over on Thursday afternoon. He and Deborah chatted for a few minutes while Deborah tried to describe what she thought Lisa had in mind.

"Her father and I want to get a nice horse for her—something sweet and gentle. She's a new rider, and we can't have her on anything too wild."

There were a lot of *hmm*s and *sure*s and one or two *of courses*. Then Deborah thanked him and hung up.

"What was all that about?" Carole asked.

"He wanted to tell me some things I should know about buying the perfect horse for 'Little Lisa,'" Deborah said.

Lisa's eyes closed to angry slits. "I hate him already," she said.

"Ah, but you mustn't let him know that," said Deborah.

Lisa opened her eyes and fluttered her lashes innocently. "I know that, Mommy," she said, like a good little girl.

"Mommy?" Max said, overhearing the end of the conversation. "I kind of like the sound of that!"

"Oh, Max!" said Deborah. "Just let us do our job, will you?"

LISA REGARDED HERSELF critically in the mirror. She opened her eyes wide and spoke. "Oh, what a beautiful horse! Can I have him, Mom? Please! Please!" she begged. It was the tenth time she'd tried this since yesterday when Deborah had agreed to let Lisa pose as her daughter. Now Lisa thought she had the whine exactly right.

She smiled at her reflection. Deborah didn't have a thing to worry about. Lisa would be perfect in her role of a horse-crazy girl. She was confident that Carole would do well in the part of the horse-crazy girl's best friend. After all, that was what she was.

She was only sorry that Stevie wouldn't be there to see it. It was such a Stevian scheme.

That made Lisa remember that Stevie had thought she'd be home from the hospital this morning. Lisa decided to call and find out.

Chad answered the phone.

"No, she's not home yet," he said. "The doctor thinks she's okay, but he said she hit her head really hard. Of course, he doesn't know what a hard head she has."

Lisa wondered briefly if there was ever a moment when Stevie and her brothers were not at odds with one another.

"Actually," Chad continued, "there may be something to be concerned about, because she still doesn't remember that it was Veronica's fault she got thrown. Like you and Carole said, when Stevie isn't ready to blame Veronica or me for everything that ever happened to her, she's not normal, right?"

"Right." Lisa had to agree.

"Anyway, the doctor said this kind of amnesia is not unusual with a concussion, but he's being cautious, so he wants her to stay there another day or two. There was something else about Frank Sinatra and Napoléon Bonaparte."

Lisa giggled. "Any doctor looking into Stevie's mind

is at a real disadvantage if she or he doesn't know what the 'normal' Stevie is like."

"I don't know what you mean," said Chad. "*Normal* is not a word I use in connection with my sister."

Lisa was tempted to mention that Stevie had said the same thing about Chad not long ago, but she really didn't want to get between the two of them. She passed up the opportunity and instead told Chad that she and Carole would visit Stevie later that day.

"Good idea," Chad said. "You two will probably do a better job of cheering her up than I can."

"Probably," Lisa said, recognizing that Chad's remark showed real concern for his sister. She and Carole always knew that the Lake children cared about one another. It was just that sometimes they had very strange ways of showing it. "I'll let you know how she is," Lisa promised. Chad thanked her and they hung up.

Lisa quickly called Carole, and the two of them agreed to meet at the hospital when visiting hours began.

At noon the girls walked together down the long polished hallway to Stevie's room. Everything was quiet inside. They tiptoed in. Stevie was asleep. Lisa put her finger to her lips. The girls each slid into a visitor's chair and waited quietly.

Carole was a little concerned that Stevie was sleeping

so soundly. She was even more concerned when she saw that Stevie's lunch tray on the rolling table next to her bed was untouched. Carole knew that Stevie's complaint about hospital food was strictly pro forma. Stevie had a stomach of iron—she could eat anything and frequently did. If she was getting fussy about food, then perhaps she really wasn't getting well.

Suddenly Stevie shifted around in her bed.

"Ouch!" she cried out.

Her eyes flew open.

"Are you okay?" Lisa asked quickly.

"Should I get the nurse?" Carole asked.

"Oh, no, I'm fine," Stevie said, smiling at her friends.

"But you yelled ouch," Lisa said.

"I guess I was just having a dream," said Stevie. She scratched her head in thought. "How's your foot?" she asked Carole.

"My foot? Nothing's wrong with it," Carole assured her.

"Well, I'm glad to hear that, because in my dream Starlight stepped on your foot and it hurt a lot. That's why I said ouch."

"You say ouch when *I* get hurt in your dreams?" Carole asked.

"That's what friends are for!" Stevie joked.

Lisa and Carole laughed. Stevie was beginning to sound more like herself.

"So what exciting things am I missing while I'm having these weird dreams in this strange hospital bed?" Stevie asked.

Carole and Lisa exchanged glances. There was a moment of doubt about whether they should tell Stevie what they were up to with Deborah. She'd be so jealous of the adventure. But lying to Stevie was hard. It was as if she had some sort of antenna that picked up evasions, especially from her two best friends. Carole nodded at Lisa, who filled in Stevie on the plan. Stevie loved it.

"You thought of that without me there?" Stevie asked.

"You were there in spirit," Lisa said.

"Right," Carole agreed. "Deborah said she wondered what you would think of doing."

"Once she suggested that, it was easy," Lisa said. "I just thought of the craziest possible plan, which was the two of us pretending we didn't know anything about horses, and then all the details fell into place."

"Oh, I wish I could go along!" Stevie said.

"Where do you want to go?" her doctor asked, hearing Stevie's remark as he walked into the room.

"It's a long story," said Stevie. "But will I be able to go to Rock Ridge on Thursday?"

"Don't even think about it," he said. With that, he brought out his penlight and went through the same exercises Lisa and Carole had seen the day before. He tapped on Stevie's knees and ankles with a little rubber hammer. He asked her a few questions.

"Who is the president?" he asked.

"John Wayne," Stevie informed him solemnly.

"Very good," he said, equally solemnly.

Stevie couldn't contain herself. She giggled.

"Just as I thought," said the doctor. "Okay, here's the story. You can go home tomorrow, but you've got to go to bed and stay in bed. You jostled your brain around rather severely, and it needs time to settle back where it belongs. Do you understand?"

"But Rock Ridge isn't that far. And it would just be a quick tr—" Stevie tried.

"Bed," the doctor said, cutting her off. "Or I'll keep you here to be sure you stay in bed."

"Home and I'll stay in bed, I promise," Stevie told him. "As long as my friends promise to tell me absolutely everything—and I mean *everything*—that happens in Rock Ridge."

"We promise," said Lisa.

"On a stack of bedpans," Carole confirmed.

"Well, that settles that," said the doctor. "I'll check on you in the morning to be sure you're okay, and I'll

36

call your parents, too. For now, you should rest." He left the room.

Carole and Lisa knew the last remark was the doctor's way of telling them it was time to leave. Now that they knew Stevie was getting better and going home, they could. They each gave her a little hug, gentle ones so they wouldn't jostle her brain any more than it had already been jostled. They left as they'd come in, on tiptoe, because Stevie's eyes were closing again.

Outside the hospital, Lisa and Carole paused to consider what they would do. There was a little time until their riding class. They decided to use the extra time in the best possible way. They were going to give Belle a complete grooming.

"It's the least we can do for Stevie while she's laid up," Carole said. Lisa agreed completely.

Fifteen minutes later, the girls were hard at work at Pine Hollow. Belle seemed happy for the company and the attention. She stood completely still while Lisa and Carole tended to her beauty needs. By the time they were done, Belle's coat was gleaming.

"Stevie would be proud of us," said Lisa.

"More important, she'd be proud of Belle," said Carole. Lisa realized that Carole was right. When it came to horses, Carole was just about always right.

"Okay, Starlight, it's your turn now," said Lisa.

She and Carole picked up the grooming gear and moved on to the gelding's stall. Starlight could be frisky under saddle, but when he was being groomed, he was usually docile as could be. A lot of horses really enjoy getting combed, brushed, and washed and being the center of attention. Starlight was no exception.

"Hi there, beautiful," Carole greeted her horse. She reached up to clip a lead rope on one side of his halter while Lisa did the same on the other side so they could cross-tie him. Starlight lifted his head and shook it vigorously, pulling his halter out of reach.

"Hey, Starlight, I've got your grooming bucket," Carole said. It was her way of assuring him that nobody was going to do anything nasty, like check his teeth or give him a shot. She held up the bucket so he could look at it.

He shook his head again, but this time he did it sideways. Lisa and Carole both managed to clip the leads on.

As the girls began the grooming, Carole knew they had been smart to cross-tie Starlight. He was in a very jumpy mood. Every time one of them touched him, he shifted away. He stepped forward, and he dodged backward the half step that the cross-ties permitted.

"Boy, is he crabby!" Carole said when he refused to lift his foot so she could pick his hoof.

"He's probably just jealous because we groomed Belle first," Lisa suggested.

Carole laughed. "Maybe," she said. If there was one thing she'd learned about horses, it was that they each had very distinct personalities—as distinct as people's personalities. That meant that they also had moods. Starlight was obviously in a bad one.

"Do you think it would be a good idea to let him stand still and get calm for a while before we finish this?" Lisa asked. "We could go change into our riding clothes while he settles down."

"That's a good idea," said Carole. "But I've started to pick his hooves, and he's refusing to let me do it. If I give in now, he might get ideas for the future. I'll just finish this and then give it a rest."

Carole stood by Starlight's left hind foot. She put her hand on his leg and bent to run her hand down to the foot. It was her signal to him that it was time to lift his foot for a hoof cleaning. He didn't lift it. She tugged as a gentle reminder. He lifted it. Then he swung it forward, out of her grasp, and clumped it back down. It landed right on her sneakered foot.

"Ouch!" she cried.

"Wow," Lisa breathed. "Just like in Stevie's dream!"

MAX TAPPED HIS riding crop impatiently against his leg. "Okay, Veronica, try that jump again," he said.

It was Wednesday. Lisa and Carole were at the afternoon class, where Max was working on jumping techniques—just as they had been doing with Stevie only a few days before when she'd fallen because of Veronica's thoughtlessness. Lisa wasn't given to thinking mean thoughts, but it occurred to her that she might feel a special piece of joy in her heart if, just by chance, Veronica were to have an accident while she was jumping.

"I hope she falls," Carole whispered to Lisa.

Lisa tried unsuccessfully to stifle a giggle. She sometimes forgot how often The Saddle Club girls had exactly the same thought at exactly the same time. It was one of the things she loved about her friends.

"Quiet," Max said in response to Lisa's laugh.

The girls wouldn't mind seeing something bad happen to Veronica, but not if it was their fault. They sat quietly and watched.

Veronica had been riding for a long time and had mastered a lot of basic and some advanced skills. She could jump well. Her horse, however, had mastered all the skills any horse could ever need, and he was an excellent jumper. Danny could have made a rank amateur look like a seasoned rider. He made Veronica look like a champion.

Danny was what some people called a push-button horse. All the rider had to do was push the right buttons and the horse did the rest. Veronica and Danny approached the jump at an even canter, and when they got three and a half feet from the fence, Danny simply rose and flew over the jump, landing smoothly, effortlessly.

Carole sighed. Lisa thought maybe it was envy, but it wasn't. It was admiration—for the horse.

"Veronica, you can't let your horse do all the work," Max snapped. "You've got to be in charge or you are not learning anything at all."

Veronica frowned, and Carole and Lisa exchanged

grins. It was fun to see Veronica get criticized by their instructor.

Max gave all the riders a short break. The riders walked their horses at a comfortable gait and chatted with one another. Max's theory was that the riders would talk about what they were learning. In the case of Lisa and Carole, he was at least half right.

"We've got to get back at her," Lisa said. "For Stevie's sake."

"But with Danny, what could go wrong?" Carole asked.

"Maybe we could startle him," said Lisa.

"He's pretty steady," Carole said.

"Maybe we could startle *her*," Lisa suggested.

"Worth a try," said Carole. "We do have to be a little careful, though. We don't want to take a chance that anything bad might happen to her horse. Danny is blameless."

"Danny is better than blameless," said Lisa. "He's to be pitied just because he belongs to Veronica! I promise not to do anything that would upset him."

The girls decided that a way to make Veronica self-conscious was to be sure everybody was staring at her. As they rode around the ring during their break, they whispered the plan to other riders. The class was more than willing to do something that might make Veronica blunder.

"Being stared at always makes people nervous," Lisa said.

It didn't make Veronica nervous. In fact, she seemed to blossom under all the attention, and it made her ride better.

"I think we just flunked 'retribution,'" Lisa whispered to Carole.

"But there *must* be a way," said Carole.

"And we'll find it, but it might take more Stevian thinking than we've put into this so far," said Lisa.

"We'll talk later," Carole whispered.

"For sure," Lisa agreed.

After class, they talked while they groomed their horses and mucked out Belle's stall. They talked about jumping; they talked about grooming. They discussed proper attire for horse shows, and they talked about how hard it was going to be for Carole to pretend to be ignorant about horses. They even talked about the fact that Phil was going gliding with his uncle Michael. They didn't talk about how they could get even with Veronica. It was unspoken between them: Stevie was the best at getting even; it wasn't the same without her, and they would just have to wait until they were with her.

"I miss her!" Lisa said, finally acknowledging what they both knew was true.

"Me too," said Carole as she put the pitchfork back where it belonged. "I wonder what we can do for her."

"I've got an idea," said Lisa. "Why don't we stop by TD's on our way to her house?"

TD's was an ice cream shop near Pine Hollow and Stevie's house. The girls often had impromptu Saddle Club meetings there, talking about the wonderful mysteries of horses while consuming their favorite sweets. One of the things about Stevie that seemed an eternal mystery to her friends was what constituted her "favorite" ice cream sundaes. *Ghastly* was one word her friends sometimes used to describe them. *Revolting* was another word they'd used from time to time. *Inventive* was what Stevie called them.

A few minutes later they ordered butter pecan ice cream with licorice bits and caramel sauce to go and pooled every cent they had on them to pay for it.

"Oh, and some chopped peanuts and marshmallow fluff," Lisa added.

Carole winced. That was how she knew they'd gotten a really good combination. If it made her stomach twinge just to hear the ingredients, it was guaranteed to please Stevie.

The girls carried their bounty proudly.

"She's going to *love* it," Lisa said.

"It's going to be her new all-time favorite," Carole agreed.

They knocked on the door. Chad invited them in and told them Stevie was in bed. "Isn't it wonderful that the doctor told her she has to *stay* there for a whole week?" he gloated.

The girls stopped by the kitchen to pick up a spoon for Stevie and then trotted upstairs. Stevie was sitting in her bed quietly. There was a television set in her room. It was off. There was a stereo next to her bed. No music was coming from it. A portable electronic game set lay silent next to her. She wasn't on the phone. She wasn't playing with her computer. She wasn't yelling at her brothers or throwing things at them.

"You okay?" Carole asked.

"Of course," said Stevie. "And I'm even better now that the two of you are here. What have you brought me?" She eyed the bag from TD's meaningfully. Lisa handed it to her proudly.

"It's our welcome-home present," she said.

Stevie beamed. She reached in and pulled out the container. Carefully she removed the lid.

"Eeuuuuuu!" she said.

"What's the matter?" Carole asked.

"What *is* this?" Stevie said, curling her lip in disgust.

"It's going to be your newest favorite," Lisa said. "It's almost the same thing you ordered just two weeks ago—"

"—and loved," Carole assured her. "Here's a spoon."

"Whatever for?" Stevie asked. "I can't eat this. Butter pecan and licorice chips? Caramel, marshmallow . . . I can't even think about it." She set the container aside and put the lid back on it. "Maybe next time you could bring me hot fudge on vanilla ice cream," she suggested.

Carole and Lisa couldn't believe their ears. There was a disgusting sundae that Stevie didn't like? "We'll remember, I promise," Carole said quickly, trying to quell the alarm in her voice. She and Lisa looked at one another. The doctor might think Stevie was better, but they knew her best. Her head was still scrambled. They were glad Stevie was going to have more rest. She needed it!

"So, have you had any more interesting dreams?" Lisa asked, changing the subject quickly as Carole spirited the offending sundae off Stevie's bedside table. She parked it on the hall table until they could take it downstairs and give it a decent burial.

"Oh, yes, but it was strange," said Stevie.

"They all are," Carole said, wiggling her sore toe uncomfortably in her sneaker.

"Actually," said Stevie, "this dream wasn't so much about the horse as it was about the horse's rider."

"Who was the rider?" Lisa asked.

"Oh, I don't know. I don't know the name of the rider or the horse. But in this case, it was about the rider and it involved a sign."

"A sign, like a mysterious symbol or something?" Carole asked. This sounded exciting.

"No, not like that at all," said Stevie. "A sign, like white with black lettering. It said Point and Laugh."

"At what?" asked Lisa.

"Beats me," said Stevie.

Carole furrowed her brow in thought. She sat down and took Stevie's hand. "Listen, there's something, actually a couple of things, that you should know about your dreams—"

Lisa didn't like the sound of this. She thought Carole meant to tell Stevie that her dreams were coming true. First Phil had been thrown from Teddy, and then Starlight had stepped on Carole's toe. Lisa didn't think it was a good idea to tell Stevie about these coincidences. Stevie's dreams were wild enough without any help from her friends.

"Right," Lisa interrupted. "What Carole is about to say is what we're both thinking. We're having a lot of fun hearing about your dreams. Every time you have an interesting one, be sure to tell us, okay?"

Carole looked as if she was about to say something, but she shut her mouth.

"Sure thing," Stevie promised. Then she stretched and yawned. "In fact, I might have a dream arriving right now . . ."

"Hi, can I come in?"

It was Phil Marsten.

"Of course you can," said Stevie. "I just told Carole and Lisa I thought you were about to walk in here."

The girls giggled. In fact, what Stevie had said was that a dream was arriving. They hadn't realized she meant the personification of a dream, one Phil Marsten.

Phil came in and perched on the chair at the foot of Stevie's bed.

"I'm so glad you're back from the hospital," he said. "I guess that means that you can ride on Saturday and we can have our jump-off, right? I hope so because I'm counting on the fact that you've had an injury to impair your abilities. I'll be a shoo-in to win, so I can take back those bribes I paid the judges."

Stevie sat up in her bed and frowned in scorn.

"Phil Marsten, I could beat you in a jump-off even if I were in a coma!" she declared. "It would take more money than you have to bribe any judges into believing that you are actually better than I am, and—"

"Calm down," Phil said. "I'm joking."

"I know." Stevie relented, smiling.

"I actually came by to tell you that maybe it's a good thing we can't do our competition this weekend because Uncle Michael says we have to leave early in the morning. We can't actually go up in the glider until noon, but we've got a drive ahead of us, and we'll have to prepare the glider when we get to Dunstable Field—that's the airport we'll use—and he says I'm going to need some preparation before our flight. His glider ID number is thirteen—he says that's for good luck! Anyway, I think he wants to give me a lesson on the ground first."

"Don't do it," Stevie said.

"Right, like I actually think you're going to be able to ride on Saturday," said Phil. "I talked to your mother last night after she talked to the doctor, and she said you're not allowed out of bed until next Tuesday and then only if the doctor says it's okay. No way I'm missing out on soaring with Uncle Michael anyway. I promise I'll tell you everything that happens. Uncle Michael says it's the best experience there is."

"No, I mean, don't do it," said Stevie. Her face was solemn and serious, something her friends didn't often see. "Not because of the jump-off, but because something is going to happen."

"You bet it is," said Phil. "What's going to happen is that we're going to fly freely for a long time. Uncle Michael says people can stay up for hours—even eight or more at a time. Isn't that something? And don't worry about safety, because gliders are very safe. They're actually safer than airplanes because they don't have engines."

"But an engine is the problem!" said Stevie, suddenly animated.

"No way," said Phil. "We'll fly the same way birds do, using currents and thermals to lift us. That's why it's called a glider or a sailplane."

"But something's wrong," Stevie said, her voice filled with concern. "It's an engine. I just know it." Her eyes closed.

Phil took her hand. "Don't worry, Stevie," he said. "There's no engine. I promise. We'll be fine."

"Maybe," Stevie conceded, her eyes still closed.

Lisa, Carole, and Phil exchanged glances.

"I think she's going to sleep for a while," said Lisa. They stood up and whispered good-byes; then they crept out of Stevie's room.

Carole picked up the spurned sundae to carry it to the kitchen. She knew better than to offer it to anybody else. She dumped it into the garbage while Lisa described its ingredients to Phil.

"And she didn't want to eat it?" he asked. "But that's right up her alley."

"She wanted hot fudge on vanilla," Lisa said. "Can you believe it?"

"I hope a week in bed will complete her transformation back to the old Stevie," said Phil.

"Me too," Carole agreed. "Until then, there's only one word to describe her behavior."

"Right," Lisa agreed.

And then all three of them said it at the same time: "*Weird.*"

"Maybe we should call her doctor," Lisa said.

"Sure, we'll just explain that we're worried about Stevie because she didn't want to eat the most repulsive sundae ever."

"He'd send *us* to our beds for a week," Carole said.

"And then I'd miss gliding," said Phil.

"And we'd miss the chance to nail a crooked horse trader," said Lisa.

52

"What's this about?" Phil asked.

Carole explained about their mission with Deborah to Rock Ridge.

"Oh, I know where that is," said Phil. "Dunstable Field is right near there. Maybe I can get Uncle Michael to fly over the guy's field."

"Great!" said Lisa. "Why don't you take a picture of the place when you're over it. It would be perfect to go with the story Deborah's writing!"

"Great idea," said Phil. "Uncle Michael always takes a camera with him. I'm sure we can do it. But in return for that, I want to hear everything that happens."

"You and Stevie both," said Carole. "At least her curiosity is still healthy!"

"Well, then there's hope," Phil said, laughing.

"YOU KNOW, THINKING about butter pecan ice cream with licorice chips makes me hungry," Carole said.

"I know what you mean," said Lisa. "It's because every other time Stevie's ordered something that revolting, you and I have gotten something delicious. I don't know about you, but buying that concoction for Stevie meant the end of my allowance, so we can't go back to TD's."

"I've discussed this phenomenon with my dad," Carole said. "It seems that the week is about three days longer than my allowance. He was surprisingly unsympathetic. He began to talk about things like 'fiscal responsibility' and 'learning to do without.' Most of the time he's the best dad in the world, but every once in a while he's more Marine than dad—if you know what I mean."

"Don't kid yourself," said Lisa. "That's as much a dad thing as it is a Marine thing. The last time I asked for a raise in my allowance, my dad started talking about budgets and doing financial projections on a computer. How much projecting can I do with the tiny allowance I get? But all is not lost. I happen to know my mother bought some vanilla ice cream when she went shopping, and we'll have a choice of chocolate or maple syrups. Okay?"

"Sounds perfect!" Carole said. "*And* the price is right!"

Fifteen minutes later they'd made their decisions. Carole was having a maple sundae. Lisa's was chocolate. They'd found some peanuts and chopped them up to put on top of the sauces. There was no whipped cream and there were no maraschino cherries. The girls didn't mind. They thought their concoctions were almost as good as what they'd have at TD's—if they could afford it.

Lisa took a drippy, gooey bite from her sundae, and when she'd swallowed, she spoke. "As long as we're eating sundaes after a riding class, then I think this is a Saddle Club meeting, even without Stevie," she said.

Carole agreed by nodding in the middle of her first bite.

"So then we have to talk about Stevie and her too-weird dreams."

"Right, like what was all that stuff about a sign—"

"Point and Laugh," Lisa reminded her.

"On a rider?" Carole asked. It was a question because it didn't make sense. Why would anyone want to laugh at someone who was riding a horse? Riding took concentration and skill. If somebody was pointing and laughing—"Oh!" she said.

"What's the matter?" asked Lisa.

"The sign!" Carole said. "It's for Veronica!"

"Right, like we could get her to point and . . . oh, no, that's not it, is it?" Lisa said.

"The sign isn't for her to read. It's for her to wear," said Carole.

"How are we going to get her to wear a sign?" asked Lisa.

"We could sort of attach it with tape?"

Lisa frowned and took another bite of her sundae. It seemed that she and Carole had been given a Stevian scheme. It was now her job, as the logical thinker, to figure out how to make it work.

She began to think out loud. "We can't have it be anything she sees coming, and it can't be anything she feels on her."

"That eliminates paper, which crinkles, and cardboard, which would bounce around."

"Cloth."

"Right, cloth," Carole agreed.

"And I think I know just exactly how to do this. Are you done with your sundae?"

"I am if you're ready to wreak revenge on Veronica," Carole announced.

The girls put their bowls in the Atwoods' dishwasher and hurried to Lisa's room.

"I have all this felt and stuff left over from craft projects," Lisa began.

Carole smiled. She had the two best friends in the world. Together, they could accomplish anything—even if it took a bonk on the head of one of them to come up with the core of a most devilish revenge scheme!

VERONICA SAUNTERED INTO the locker room on Thursday morning. Class would begin in ten minutes. All of the other students had arrived a half hour earlier to change their clothes and tack up their horses. Veronica didn't worry about anything as boring as tacking up her horse. That was what stable hands were for. All she had to do was change into her riding clothes.

"Hi, Veronica," Carole greeted her.

"Oh, hello," Veronica said coolly. She never could understand those Saddle Club girls. Most of the time they were rude to her, but every once in a while they would behave nicely. Veronica supposed it was for the obvious reason. They were rude because they were jealous, and they were nice because they were hoping to get in good with her so that some of her taste would rub off on them. She smiled at Carole, knowing that her greeting was going to be the brightest part in poor Carole's otherwise dull day.

"New clothes?" Lisa asked, looking at the zippered bag that Veronica carried.

"Yes," said Veronica. "Mother thought my old ones were getting tattered." *Of course Lisa must have noticed that*, Veronica thought. She was probably wondering what happened with Veronica's old clothes. She probably wished Veronica would offer them to her. Veronica knew that her castoffs were actually in better condition than the riding habits Lisa usually wore. And as for Stevie—well, the less said about her outfits the better. Although Veronica had no intention of donating her old clothes to Lisa, it wouldn't hurt to give the girl a few pointers.

"We got these at The Saddlery," said Veronica. "You know, they'll put anything out on the rack there, but if you ask, the tailor can make you really first-rate clothes.

I used to think we had to go shopping in the city to get quality. But we actually do almost as well with the custom-made things at The Saddlery. I'm sure they could do something for you."

"Oh, wow," said Lisa. "Do you think so? Would they actually be able to make something as nice for me as they do for you?"

"I don't see why not," said Veronica.

"Well, please do show me your new clothes," Lisa said eagerly. "I'm always fascinated with the outfits you wear. Such style, such taste, such colors!"

Lisa sounded almost breathless with excitement. Veronica was pleased. The fact was she'd often thought that Lisa seemed to have pretty good taste in clothes, so it didn't surprise her to find that Lisa had, apparently, been modeling her own wardrobe after Veronica's.

It only took Veronica a minute to pull on her new, soft riding pants. They were an elegant doeskin brown with leather patches inside the knees. They fit her legs sleekly and flattered her figure. Veronica showed Lisa that the skills of the little old tailor at The Saddlery were really quite adequate.

"I've got to say I'm impressed," Lisa remarked. "Can I see your new jacket, too?"

Veronica slipped it on. It annoyed her that she had on an old shirt—something she'd already worn twice.

When she got into new clothes, she liked to be in new clothes from the skin out. Still, the shirt was good quality, and the jacket's tailoring complemented it and the new breeches perfectly.

"Ohhhh," said Lisa. "The lines! The seams! The fabric!"

Veronica didn't even try to hide her pleasure at Lisa's compliments. "I'm sure that if you tell your mother how good this old man is, she'd consider having him whip one of these up for you, too," she said.

"I don't know, but I sure am going to ask her!" Lisa said. "Now let me see it from the rear. The rear is always so important. It's the impression you leave people with, you know?"

"Yes, I know," said Veronica. She turned.

"Oh, wow," said Lisa. "It's . . . it's—uh-oh."

"What?" asked Veronica.

"Oh, nothing," said Lisa.

"You saw something. What's wrong?" Veronica asked.

"Well, I think he left a—here, let me see. Move back here into the light." Veronica stepped back. "Oh, it's just a thread or something. I think I can get it. Stand still."

"I didn't see anything when I picked it up," Veronica said. "I tried it on, of course."

"Of course," said Lisa. "I think I have it . . ."

Veronica felt a tug, then some pressure. "What is it?"

"I've got it," said Lisa. "All done. It was just a thread. It made ever so slight a wrinkle in the jacket. Here, let me smooth it for you."

She passed her hands across Veronica's shoulders several times, smoothing out the wrinkles. Veronica was steaming. How could that careless old man at that second-rate tack shop have the gall to leave a thread on her jacket?

"Oh, Veronica, it's just perfect!" Lisa said.

"You think so?"

"Well, it is now," Lisa said. "And don't worry about that. It was just a tiny thread. It could have happened to anybody."

But it shouldn't have happened to me, Veronica thought. She'd have a word with that stupid old man next time she went to The Saddlery. The thought made her happy. Perhaps it was time to go see if that lazy stable hand had tacked up Danny.

"Oh, Red, are you finished yet?" she called loudly as she strutted out of the locker area, perfectly dressed—at least as far as Lisa and Carole were concerned. They could barely contain their giggles until Veronica was out of earshot.

"You were perfect!" Carole said, hugging her friend. "An Oscar-winning performance! 'Ooooh, Veronica!'" she mimicked. "'The lines, the seams, the fabric!'"

"And she actually believed me!" Lisa preened.

"Of course she did," said Carole. "That girl's outsized ego needs constant feeding. She believes every compliment, no matter how outrageous."

"Well, let's see how she likes being the center of attention today," Lisa said.

The girls followed Veronica's route out of the locker area and went to get their own horses, tacked up by their own hands.

The first snort of laughter came from Meg Durham. The second came from Betsy Cavanaugh.

"Hey, look!" Lorraine Olson said, pointing at Veronica. Then she started laughing, too.

Carole looked over the top of Starlight's stall. There was Veronica, standing next to Danny, ready to mount her Thoroughbred. She was dressed in shiny black leather boots, doeskin-colored riding pants, a simple but elegant shirt, and a perfectly tailored black broadcloth jacket. To complete the outfit, she had a white band of cotton across her back with black lettering that read Point and Laugh.

Everybody at Pine Hollow seemed only too willing to accommodate the request.

Veronica looked annoyed and upset.

"Just *what* is so funny," she asked, stamping a foot. "Can someone please let me in on the joke?"

That only made everyone laugh harder. Finally a red-faced Veronica yanked on Danny's reins and stalked out of the barn, with the horse walking behind her.

Lisa and Carole exchanged high fives over the wall between their horses' stalls.

"Who says we can't pull off a great practical joke when Stevie's not here?" Lisa asked.

Carole just grinned.

CAROLE AND LISA were still beaming with pride at their accomplishment when Deborah told them it was time to leave for Rock Ridge.

"What are you two grinning about?" Deborah asked them as she pulled out of Pine Hollow's driveway.

"Oh, just a minor victory in defense of a defenseless friend," Lisa answered. She was trying to sound as innocent as possible.

"Does this have anything to do with what Max was trying to tell me about in the tack room before we left?" Deborah asked.

"Max? Why, what was he saying?" Carole asked.

"He wasn't saying much," said Deborah. "He was *trying* to tell me something, but he was laughing too hard to explain what it was."

Carole and Lisa exchanged glances. Max hadn't given the slightest indication that he'd even noticed the sign on Veronica's back. He'd ignored it so completely that they'd thought perhaps he actually hadn't seen it.

"Maybe he did see it," said Carole.

"But probably not," Lisa said. "It's just that, well . . ." She and Carole looked at one another, and then they couldn't keep from laughing, just one more time.

"I know that laugh," Deborah said with certainty. "It's exactly the same laugh Max couldn't hold in. I guess I'll just have to ask him about it later, huh?"

"Good idea," Lisa said. "For now, maybe I should try practicing my part, *Mom*."

"That sounds even stranger to me than it must to you," Deborah said.

"It sure does, *Mom*," Lisa said. It didn't sound any better the second time. "Say, *Mom*, would you buy me a horse, please, please, please?"

"Much better," Deborah said. "Now you sound authentic."

Lisa thought it would be a good idea to call Deborah Mom all the way to Rock Ridge. At the same time,

Carole practiced calling her Mrs. Hale. She'd never called her anything but Deborah before, but they'd all decided Mrs. Hale sounded more authentic.

"Oh, look, Mrs. Hale," said Carole, trying out her role, "isn't that Dunstable Field? That's where Phil Marsten's uncle Michael keeps his glider."

"Oh, really? I guess it is a small world, because I happen to know that that's where Veronica's father keeps the bank's airplane."

"The bank has an *airplane?*" Lisa said. Then, to be safe, she added, "Mom?"

"Yes, it does. I learned that when I was doing some research on local companies and the perks that their top executives get. Mr. diAngelo claims that he keeps the plane for company business, and every time he has a business trip, he does use it. But he also uses it when he goes to play golf or if he and Mrs. diAngelo want to go to New York for the weekend. He's very careful, though. When he goes to play golf, he goes with customers. When he and Mrs. diAngelo go to New York, he does business there. It's not unethical, exactly."

"Funny that Veronica never mentioned it to us, Mrs. Hale," Carole said. "She rarely misses an opportunity to boast about something."

"I guess she doesn't get to ride in it much," said Deborah.

Carole realized that was true. She remembered the time Mr. and Mrs. diAngelo had gone for a long golfing trip over Thanksgiving and had left Veronica to celebrate the holiday with the servants. Perhaps Veronica didn't talk about the plane because she resented the fact that she couldn't take advantage of it.

"Poor little rich girl," Carole said.

"Right, like my heart breaks for her," Lisa added.

"It's time to stop thinking about Veronica," said Deborah.

"What's more important than that?" Lisa teased.

"Well, my little sweetie pie, we're about to arrive at Mickey Denver's farm."

"Oh, right, Mom," said Lisa. "And I want a horse, any horse."

"And I'm here to help you buy a really *pretty* one," said Carole. "Right, Mrs. Hale?"

"Right, Carole," said Deborah. She flipped on her turn signal and drove up a long driveway to a lovely horse farm. The farm was in a valley with mountains at the far end, including the famous outcropping of rocks known as Rock Ridge. The barn was near the neat farmhouse. It was surrounded by paddocks and schooling

67

rings. In each paddock were horses, some grazing lazily, some playing and frolicking.

"Perfect," Carole said. "If I decide to have a horse farm, I want it to look exactly like this, Mrs. Hale."

"But let's hope you have a better reputation as a horse trader than I suspect we'll find Mr. Denver has earned."

"Oh, Mommy! Mommy! Look at the horsie!" Lisa said.

"Too young," said Deborah.

"Wow, Mom! Look at all the horses!" Lisa tried a second time.

"Much better," said Deborah. She pulled the car to a stop at the barn and opened the door.

A middle-aged man wearing jeans and riding boots was right by the entrance to the barn. He walked up to the car.

"Ah, you must be Mrs. Hale!" he said, greeting Deborah warmly as they got out of the car.

"I am," said Deborah. "And this is my daughter, Lisa, and her friend, Carole. I should remind you that we've just started looking for a horse for Lisa, and we're not likely to buy one today. It's just that you were recommended to us—"

"You don't have to say another word," said Mr. Denver. "I'm no hard-pitch salesman. My job is to match the horse to the rider, and if there's any doubt in your mind, then I haven't done my job right and you shouldn't be buying from my stock anyway. Now, tell me, uh—Lizzie, is it?"

"Lisa," she said.

"Right, Lisa," he said. "Have you been riding long?"

"Just a little while," said Lisa. "And I really love it. I just want a pretty horse that's all mine. Mom, I promise I'm going to love it to pieces! Have you got any white ones?"

"White? Well, if that's what you want, then that's what you must have!" he said.

"One with a silky mane," said Carole. She nearly choked on the words as she uttered them, though. The problem was that she couldn't think of anything less important about a horse than what color his coat was or if his mane was "silky." Manes became silky when they were properly brushed and combed.

"A silky mane, too?" Mr. Denver said. "Boy, you girls sure know exactly what you want, don't you? You must have been doing a lot of studying!"

"We sure have," Lisa said.

"Well, I think this is your lucky day," said Mr. Denver. "Because I happen to have just exactly the horse you are describing. Mind you, this horse has been in my family for a long time. She was my daughter's favorite horse when she was learning. She rode her in dozens of shows—do you ride in shows?" he asked Lisa.

"Well, I'd really *like* to," Lisa said. "Would I win ribbons with this horse?"

"You'd have to buy a whole glass cabinet for your ribbons, Liz—er, Lisa," he said.

"Blue ones?" Lisa asked.

"Sure thing, sweetheart," said Mr. Denver.

"Oh, Mom, I want to see this horse!" said Lisa. Her voice was eager and breathless—just the way she wanted to sound.

"Then you shall," said Deborah. "Let's meet him, Mr. Denver."

"Her," Mr. Denver said, correcting Deborah's assumption. "Blondie is a *her*," he explained unnecessarily.

"Oh, you mean, like a *mare*?" Carole asked.

"Wow, you know that term?" Mr. Denver said.

Carole swallowed her pride and nodded, smiling broadly at the man.

Mr. Denver took the girls and Deborah through the barn and out to a paddock on the far side. And there was Blondie. Mr. Denver whistled. The horse's ears pricked up. He whistled again.

"Here, girl," he said. "There are some nice young ladies to see you!" He kept talking and whistling while the horse came over to them.

Carole and Lisa both studied everything they could about the mare while she approached them. The hard part was that they didn't want to look as if they were studying the mare with practiced eyes. They wanted to *look* as if all they cared about was a white coat and a silky mane.

"This way, girl," Mr. Denver said. "See how pretty her coat is. Now, she's been out in the field, so there's some dirt on her, but you won't see a prettier white than that coat, I promise you. And the mane? It's like pure silk!"

Blondie arrived and waited obediently while Mr. Denver gave her a little piece of carrot. Carole tried not to frown. Giving a horse a treat was okay as long as the horse had done something to deserve it. Walking over to her owner didn't really qualify in Carole's book. She covered her frown with a smile.

"Oh, she's beautiful!" said Carole.

"Mom, I've just got to ride her!" said Lisa. "Can I, Mr. Denver?" she asked.

"Well, I wouldn't think of selling a horse to someone without letting her ride it first. Of course you can. You wait just a minute and I'll put the tack on Blondie—you know what tack is, don't you?" he asked.

"Is that, like, the saddle and the rein thing?" Lisa asked.

"Very bright girl you've got here, Mrs. Hale," said Mr.

Denver. "That's right. Tack is the saddle and the rein thing. It'll just take me a minute," he said. With that, he took Blondie by her halter and led her into the barn.

"The *rein thing?*" Carole whispered to Lisa.

"So far, you're perfect," Deborah told the girls. "Both of you. I personally *loved* the 'rein thing.' Max is going to love it when I tell him, too."

Minutes later Mr. Denver arrived with a fully tacked Blondie. In fact, she had more than the usual amount of tack on. She had a lead rope snapped onto her bridle— now known as the rein thing.

"Since you're a beginner, I am going to hold on to the lead rope, but you get the reins and you can take her wherever you want to go, as long as I can go along, too."

"I never have a leash thing on when I ride in class!" Lisa protested. "I don't want one now. I can do fine without it. Mom, tell him!" Lisa whined.

"Oh, I don't know," said Deborah. "This horse seems like she's got a lot of get-up-and-go. I'd hate to see her run away with you."

Carole looked at the tame, plodding old mare they were discussing and wondered how Deborah could say that with a straight face.

"Your mother's right," said Mr. Denver. "Now, let me help you into the saddle."

This was a tricky part because climbing into a horse's

saddle was one of the first things all of Max's students learned to do, and they learned to do it well. It would be a dead giveaway if Lisa did one of her usual snappy mounts. Carole held her breath. She needn't have bothered.

"Which side?" Lisa asked.

"Uh, over here," said Mr. Denver, smiling broadly. In a minute, he'd given Lisa a hand up into the saddle, helping her get her right leg over the old horse's broad back.

And then the ride began. He led Blondie over a well-worn path that circled her paddock. He walked around once, and then, at Lisa's insistence, he let the mare trot. It was an effort, both for Blondie and for Mr. Denver. Lisa, however, was in her element.

"Oh, Mom! Blondie is the perfect horse! I can't believe we found her the first place we looked! Her walk is so gentle, and her trot! Well, I never felt a smooth trot like this before!"

Carole had known Lisa was a good actress, but she'd never known she was this good. She even managed to post on the wrong diagonal! That was something Max's riders learned never to do by their third lesson.

The third time around the circle, Blondie was walking again, and seemed glad of it. That gave Lisa a chance to look around the farm a little more. The mountains were very dramatic, and Rock Ridge itself was stark and beautiful. Then something moved in the air by the mountain. Lisa squinted to see what it was. It was a glider—just like the one Phil would be in in two days. Suddenly Lisa was very glad she was sitting in the saddle of an earthbound horse. The glider seemed very small and fragile compared to the mountain behind it.

"So, Mrs. Hale, is it time for us to make a deal?" Mr. Denver asked, drawing Blondie to a halt right in front of Deborah.

"Well, if Lisa thinks this is the perfect horse for her, then I guess we should—um—once I've had a vet check her over."

Mr. Denver shook his head disapprovingly. "I thought you wanted to *buy*, not haggle," he said.

"Oh, we do," Deborah assured him. "It's just that I thought it would be a good idea if a vet—"

"Mrs. Hale, you obviously don't know much about horse trading, do you?"

"Well, no," Deborah said uncertainly.

"The fact is that I have a vet out here to my ranch three times a week to look after one thing or another. I own somewhere between forty and fifty horses, so the vet spends a lot of time here. He's never once had to give any treatment to Blondie."

"She's that healthy?" Deborah said.

"Not one problem," said Mr. Denver. "And I'd stake my reputation on it."

He doesn't know how right he is! thought Carole.

"Look, I can't tell you what to do or not do, but this here is a fine piece of horseflesh, and if young Lizzie here doesn't buy her, somebody else will. It doesn't really make any difference to me. I'll get my price. But when I saw the smile on your little girl's face—and what a pretty smile that is—I just knew it was a match, the kind of match I insist on when I sell a horse."

"But Mr. Denver—" said Deborah.

"*Mom,*" said Lisa, coming in on cue. "This is the one. I just know it! I have to have her! I promise she's perfect, and anybody can see she's in great health! Please, Mom?"

Deborah sighed. "Well, if you say so, darling," she began. "But we did make a deal. Remember?"

"I remember," Lisa said, relenting. Then she turned to explain to Mr. Denver. "Mom and I promised Dad that we wouldn't make any snap decisions. Even when I know I have exactly the perfect horse, I promised that I would wait for two days to be sure. You can understand that, can't you?"

Mr. Denver shrugged. "It's up to you," he said. "I know a good match when I see one, but if you need to wait a few days, you wait a few days. However, I'm telling you—if somebody else comes along with cash in hand before you do, well, I'm just going to have to sell her."

"Mom!" Lisa wailed.

"It was our deal," Deborah said firmly.

Reluctantly, and poorly, Lisa dismounted. She made a display of hugging the horse and promising she'd be back. Mr. Denver smiled insincerely. Then he held the car door open for Deborah.

"See you in a few days," he said.

"I suspect you will," Deborah said. "I'll call you first."

"Right," he said.

He closed the car door smartly and waved to the girls as they drove away.

"Don't say a thing until we are out the gate of this place," Deborah said through clenched teeth. "I don't know if he can read lips."

Lisa and Carole remained silent for a whole thirty seconds. As soon as they were off Mr. Denver's property, they both began howling with laughter.

"Boy, are you right! This man is a crook through and through!" Lisa said.

"I thought so. It was a giveaway when he said he didn't want me to have a vet check the horse. Right?"

"Right for starters," Lisa said. "No legitimate dealer

would ever try to talk a client out of getting a horse vet-checked."

"But what would a vet find wrong with that sweet mare anyway?" Deborah asked.

"Oh, not much," said Carole. "Unless you count blindness."

MRS. DIANGELO LEANED FORWARD and reached for the little silver bell that rested on the mahogany dinner table in front of her. She picked it up and rang it gently. The maid appeared from the kitchen and began serving dinner to Veronica and her parents.

"Did you have a good day, dear?" Mrs. diAngelo asked her husband.

"It was difficult, as usual," he said, sighing. "I had to fly to Richmond and meet with the state banking lobbyists. Then, on the way back, there was a storm system we had to let pass before we could take off. We were an hour late getting back to Dunstable."

"That was no worse than my day," said Mrs. di-Angelo. "I had a terrible row with a woman at the dry cleaner's. They delivered my silk blouse with a note saying they couldn't remove one of the stains. Imagine!"

"Oh dear," said Mr. diAngelo. He took a sip of his consommé. "And what about you, Veronica? How are you progressing with your photographic project?"

"Not too well," she admitted. "I'm having a lot of trouble finding a worthy subject."

"Veronica, you have a very expensive camera. I'm sure you can take a really good photograph with it."

Veronica swallowed a taste of her soup. She knew her father was right, in a way. He'd bought her the best camera available. Anything she took a picture of seemed to come out well. But it wasn't just the technical quality of the photograph that counted.

"It's not so much the photograph as the subject matter, Daddy," she said. "I spent a lot of time last weekend at Pine Hollow trying to find something worthwhile, but all I got was a girl falling off her horse. That's hardly an example of skill, and that's what the photograph is supposed to show. It all seems so silly to me. Do I really have to do this, Daddy?"

Mr. diAngelo put down his spoon. "Yes, Veronica, you do," he said. "In the first place, you said you'd like to have a trip to Rome—"

79

"But you can afford to pay for it . . . ," Veronica protested.

"Of course I can," said Mr. diAngelo. "But that's not the point. You need to learn what it's like to earn something. I've given you all the help I can by buying you the camera. You have to do the rest. I'm certain you can do it, too."

"Well, I'm sure I can," said Veronica. "After all, all the other kids who enter the contest are just going to be sending in pictures of their pets or their parents or their baby brothers and sisters. I'm sure the store will be only too happy to see what I send them, when I figure out what would truly be different. But everything I've thought of so far is pretty dull or else hasn't worked."

The maid reappeared to remove the soup plates and then to serve the lamb chops, asparagus, and lyonnaise potatoes. None of the diAngelos spoke as dinner was served. They didn't like to talk about personal matters in front of the servants. Veronica's mother had explained to her at an early age that one never could tell what servants might gossip about. When the door shut silently behind the maid, the conversation picked up again.

"I mean, you talk about how difficult and boring it was for you to have to fly all the way to Richmond today, but that sounds much more interesting than the day I had," said Veronica.

Mr. diAngelo took a taste of his lamb chop and made a slight face. "I told you, I like it pink, not overdone," he said to Mrs. diAngelo.

"I told the cook that four times," Mrs. diAngelo said. "I guess I'll just have to fire her."

"But Daddy," asked Veronica, "wasn't there anything interesting about your day?"

"Well, the clouds outside the airplane were quite lovely. The storm cloud particularly. Of course, we were miles away from it, but you can see great distances when you're in the sky. It's quite spectacular sometimes."

"Wow! That's it!" said Veronica.

"What's it?" her mother asked.

"I should go up in the plane and take pictures from up there. It's got to be more interesting than baby brothers and pets wearing baseball caps. It's certainly more interesting than a rider falling off a horse!"

"But the theme has to do with skill," Mr. diAngelo reminded her. "What about riding in the plane relates to that?"

"The skill of the pilot, of course," Veronica replied.

Mrs. diAngelo smiled with pride. "I'm sure that's an excellent idea," she said to her husband. "You can arrange that, can't you?"

"Well, the plane does belong to the bank," Mr. diAngelo said.

"But Daddy," Veronica asked, "didn't you tell me that the pilot needs to have more flying time to maintain his qualifications? What could be better than letting him have extra time in the air while he gets to do a favor for his boss by taking his boss's daughter up for a ride? What could be better for him than that?"

"Well, Hubert did mention something about wanting more flying hours, yes," said Mr. diAngelo.

Mrs. diAngelo rang the bell to have the maid clear the table. Before the maid came into the dining room, Mrs. diAngelo spoke rapidly to her husband.

"Oh, darling, don't be a stick-in-the-mud. This will be a perfect opportunity for the pilot—what's his name? Herbert?"

"Hubert."

"Whatever, Hubert. Veronica is right. And she'll be able to take some photographs up there that will be far superior to whatever else gets sent into that contest. How could you deny your daughter this opportunity?"

"Well, maybe you're right," Mr. diAngelo said.

The kitchen door swung open and the maid came in.

"Please clear the table and bring us our dessert," said

Mrs. diAngelo. "Oh, and when you go back into the kitchen, tell the cook she's fired."

"Yes, ma'am," said the maid.

Once again, everything was peaceful in the diAngelo household.

"HELLO, VERONICA," LISA greeted her the next day at their riding class. "Wearing the same old jacket again?"

"Yes," Veronica said sweetly. She smiled at Lisa, then walked past her without another word.

Clearly Veronica was not going to give Lisa the satisfaction of admitting that she knew Lisa had bested her with the flattery and the sign on her back the previous day. It was all right. Lisa knew and Carole knew and everybody else knew. That was quite enough. Even though Stevie was still in bed recovering from her concussion, Lisa could almost feel her spirit. Lisa could let Veronica try to pretend the sign on her back hadn't happened, but she couldn't let Veronica get away scot-free.

"How's your little photographic project coming along?" Lisa asked with as much condescension as she could muster.

"Just fine," said Veronica. "Wonderfully, in fact. Just yesterday I came up with an idea that is sure to win me first place."

"What's that?" Lisa asked.

"Skyscapes," said Veronica.

"How nice," said Lisa, hoping she sounded as if she didn't mean it.

"Yes," Veronica agreed. She wafted out of the locker area.

Lisa looked over to where Carole was straightening her blouse and tucking it into her riding pants. "I think I'll do better if I just don't speak to her again, don't you?"

"I always feel that way," Carole said. "But there is a person I do want to speak to, and that's Stevie. Are we on for visiting her after class?"

"Definitely," said Lisa. "There's so much to tell her, and it'll be great to see her because by now she must be feeling better, don't you think?"

"And acting more normal, I hope," Carole said.

Two hours later, when class was over and they'd

groomed Starlight and Prancer and looked after Belle, the girls tromped over to Stevie's house.

"How's she doing?" Carole asked Stevie's twin brother, Alex, when he opened the door for them.

"The doctor was here," he said. "He told Mom that Stevie's making a wonderful recovery."

"Great," said Carole.

"But the problem is that he didn't know Stevie before she got hit on the head."

"Still?"

"See for yourself," Alex said, inviting them to go upstairs.

"The story about Veronica's sign will do wonders for her," Carole said to Lisa.

"And wait until we tell her about Blindie—I mean, Blondie," said Lisa.

She crossed her fingers for luck as they went into Stevie's room. Everything *seemed* normal. Stevie was clearly glad to have them there, and she greeted them warmly. She did want to hear about everything that had been going on. Lisa began with the story of the sign on Veronica's back.

". . . and then I told her she had a loose thread on the back of her jacket," said Lisa.

"She played Veronica like a violin!" said Carole.

"Well, Veronica's easy to read," Lisa said humbly. "Anyway, while I pulled the imaginary thread off her jacket, I put a sign across her back—just like in your dream."

"You should have seen her in class!" Carole said. "Everybody got it. They all laughed and pointed. It was hysterical!"

Lisa giggled. "The look on Veronica's face was priceless! Of course, she couldn't admit that anything was going on. She just kept a straight face and went through the entire class with everyone laughing and pointing!"

Stevie looked a little confused. "Sure everybody laughed and pointed. There was a sign on Veronica's back that told them to. Why wouldn't they?"

Carole gulped. This definitely was *not* the old Stevie. The old Stevie would have been laughing as hard as her friends. What had come over her? It was eerie and a little frightening. Carole could tell that nothing she and Lisa said about the event was going to make Stevie see any humor in it. She decided to change the subject.

"And then after class, we went with Deborah to the horse farm in Rock Ridge."

"The guy wants to sell me this sweet horse. Her name is Blondie. And he let me ride—"

"She's blind," said Stevie.

"Right, exactly," said Lisa. "Both Carole and I knew it the moment he had to keep talking to get her to come over—" Lisa's jaw dropped when she registered what Stevie had said. "But I didn't tell you that part yet."

"How did you know?" Carole asked, stunned.

"I just did," said Stevie. "It had to be."

"Did you talk to Deborah?" Lisa asked suspiciously.

"No, did she call me?" Stevie asked.

"That's what I wanted to know," said Lisa. This conversation was getting creepy!

"Max must have told you then," said Carole.

"He's coming over here, you know," said Stevie.

"He is?" Lisa asked. It was funny, but Max hadn't said anything about that to her or Carole.

The doorbell rang. A few seconds later, Max and Deborah came into Stevie's room. Max was carrying a bouquet of daisies. Mrs. Lake brought a vase to put them in and set it on the windowsill in Stevie's room.

"We were just telling Stevie about Blondie," said Carole. "I guess you told her about the blindness when you called, right?" she asked.

"We didn't call," said Deborah. "I hope it's okay that we just dropped in."

"Of course it is, Mom," said Stevie.

Both Lisa and Carole smiled. And then, startled, they

each realized that they hadn't mentioned anything to Stevie about the fun they'd had calling Deborah Mom and Mrs. Hale.

"I see you girls have told Stevie about our beautiful mother-and-daughter bonding experience," Deborah said, grinning at Lisa.

"As a matter of fact, we hadn't gotten around to that part of the story yet," Lisa said.

"But you told her about calling me Mom, right?" asked Deborah, the grin slowly fading off her face.

"As a matter of fact," said Carole, "we hadn't."

Deborah and Max exchanged goggle-eyed looks.

"Stevie, how did you kn—" Max started to say, but Deborah put a hand on his arm and he stopped talking.

"Well, I'll tell you one thing for sure about Blondie," said Stevie, who didn't seem to notice the sudden air of tension in the room.

"What's that?" Lisa asked.

"The horse has vision," said Stevie.

"No, she's blind. I know it," said Carole. "I mean, I didn't do any tests like waving my hand in front of her face, because that would have been too obvious, but she's blind. Of that I'm sure."

"Me too," Lisa said.

"She has vision," Stevie said solemnly. "There's more

than one kind of vision, you know. Now, if you'll excuse me, I'm getting a little tired and I think I need to take a nap. Do you mind?"

"Oh, not at all," Lisa said. "We definitely want you to get all the rest you need. We'll see you tomorrow, okay?"

"Okay," Stevie said sleepily, slipping down under her covers while her eyes closed. She was asleep before they were out of her room.

Carole, Lisa, Max, and Deborah were silent until they reached the Lake kitchen. Mrs. Lake was there making dinner for the family.

"What do you think?" Mrs. Lake asked. She looked hopefully at four of the people who knew Stevie best.

"Strange," Carole said.

"Un-Stevian," said Lisa.

"But—uh—perceptive," said Max.

"Very," said Deborah.

"I've tried to explain it to the doctor," said Mrs. Lake. "He just doesn't seem to understand."

"Stevie's not easy to explain," Max said sympathetically.

"Even when she's healthy," said Carole.

And that seemed to sum it up for all of them.

PHIL FELT A twinge of excitement in the pit of his stomach. "I can't believe I'm actually going up in your glider," he told Uncle Michael.

"We've been talking about this for a long time, haven't we?" Uncle Michael asked.

"It seems like it's been hundreds of years, but I suspect it's just been more like three."

"Since that's exactly how long I've owned my two-seater, I think you're right," Uncle Michael said. "We just had to wait until you got to be what your mother thought was 'old enough.'"

He turned the car off the main road, following signs to

Dunstable Field. The area had a small collection of large, low buildings. A wind sock next to the main building showed a gentle, steady wind from the west. A dozen or so small planes were parked nearby. To the side a long strip of roadway served as the parking area for the gliders. Uncle Michael drove around the main building and off to the side road where his glider waited.

"There's always a lot of work to do before we take off," said Uncle Michael, parking the car.

"That's one thing soaring has in common with horse-back riding, then," said Phil. "I think it's usually about two hours' worth of work in and around the stable for each hour in the saddle. I don't mind, though. Anything to do with horses is fun."

"That's the way I feel about gliders," said Uncle Michael, smiling at Phil.

The two walked over to the glider. Uncle Michael put out his hand to touch the plane as they neared it. The motion made Phil think of the affectionate touch he gave Teddy every time he was going for a ride. He tried it himself. The glider was made of a lightweight carbon fiber. It was sleek and shiny. Compared with the airplanes behind the main building, the part of the craft that held the pilots was very compact, but the wingspan was several times larger.

92

Uncle Michael removed the protective canvas cover and then offered Phil a sponge and a bucket of water.

"First, we wash," he announced.

"Well, there's one difference between gliding and riding," said Phil. "I usually give Teddy a quick grooming before we ride, but the really good grooming comes after." He took the sponge and began wiping one of the glider's elegant wings. The white surface was so shiny he could see his reflection in it.

"We want to try to remove anything that would spoil the lift or create drag and slow down the craft while we're in the air," Uncle Michael explained, wiping the other wing. "Also, it's an opportunity to check the airframe to be sure the whole thing is in good condition."

They wiped and they dried.

Uncle Michael then went through a check routine on all of the equipment, including the batteries, radio, instruments, parachutes, controls, a canteen of water, granola bars, and first aid kit.

"Boy, it's like we're going up for days instead of for a few hours," said Phil.

"And if you were just going for a five-minute ride, wouldn't you want your horse to have all his tack, just as you'd want if you were going for a four-hour trail ride?"

"Check," Phil said.

"Ah, you're getting the language," Uncle Michael said, smiling.

"Roger that," Phil informed him.

"Now I need to check on the local weather outlook," said Uncle Michael. He switched on the radio and called the tower. While the tower checked the weather, Uncle Michael told Phil why he needed to know the forecast.

"Gliders go up and stay up chiefly because of one thing," he said, "and that's temperature. The slightest difference—a degree or two of warmth—will create what we call thermals, or patches of rising air. You remember that warm air rises?"

Phil nodded. He'd learned about that in science class.

"What a glider pilot wants is to be in the middle of the warm air that's rising. That gives us what we call lift. In general, what I want to do is to get the plane in an area of lift and take advantage of that by going up in circles in the area. Once I've gotten as high as I want— perhaps ten to fifteen thousand feet—then I can go forward. When luck and the weather are with me, I'll meet up with lots more thermals that will keep me at that height, or, if I do lose some altitude, I'll find more lift when I need to go higher."

"Boy, if the weather stays right, you can go on forever, then, can't you?" Phil asked.

"Not exactly," said Uncle Michael. "For one thing, as

the sun goes down, the thermals disappear. For another thing, while there are thermals that give lift, like most good things, there is an opposite. That's known as sink. Sink will bring you down as fast as lift will raise you up. Wherever you go, whatever you do in a glider, you've always got to leave room for sink. This is especially true where we'll be flying today, over these beautiful mountains. Here, we get lift from thermals, but we also get lift from the updrafts that occur when wind hits a mountainside and is deflected upward. That can be perilous, however, since the currents that pass over the top of the ridges tend to drop quite suddenly on the other side."

"Sink," said Phil.

"Big sink," agreed Uncle Michael. "So we fly carefully when we have to be near the mountaintops. There are a number of precautions glider pilots take to avoid risks. One of them is that one glider passing another near a ridge never, never passes on the outside of the other. That might tend to force the other glider closer to the mountain, where the winds are unpredictable, dangerous, and—"

"Phil? Is that Phil *Marsten*?"

Phil turned to see who was interrupting his conversation with Uncle Michael.

"Veronica?" he asked, surprised. "What are you doing here?"

Veronica smoothed her already impeccably smooth blouse and blinked sweetly.

"Why, I was about to ask you the same question!" she cooed.

"Uncle Michael, this is Veronica diAngelo. She rides at the same stable as my girlfriend, Stevie Lake," Phil said. He wouldn't normally have bothered to explain that Stevie was his girlfriend. Uncle Michael certainly didn't need to know it, but from the way Veronica was blinking at him wide-eyed, it seemed to Phil that *she* needed a reminder that Phil had a girlfriend.

"Ooooh, are you going to go flying in that thing?" she asked, pointing at Uncle Michael's glider.

"Yes," Phil said, sighing.

"I'm going for a ride in Daddy's plane," Veronica said, answering a question that hadn't been asked. "It's that big one over there." She pointed to a plane that was parked behind the main building. Next to the plane a man was waving at Veronica, telling her it was time for them to take off. Veronica waved back at him, as if it were a greeting. The man began walking toward Veronica and Phil. "Daddy's pilot, Hubert, is taking me up for a ride. It'll be the first time I get to go up in the *private* plane. I just know it's going to be great."

"I'm sure it is," Phil said. He had long since learned

that it didn't pay to engage in any conversation with Veronica. The less said to or by her, the better.

"Our tow is about ready," said Uncle Michael. "Shall we go? Nice meeting you, Veronica."

A small golf cart arrived to pull the glider onto the runway, where the tow plane would take them up as high as they needed to go to find thermals—approximately two thousand feet.

Ten minutes later, Phil had clipped on his parachute and was in the backseat of the glider. He fastened his safety harness securely and closed the clear plastic canopy over his head. Uncle Michael was in front of him. They finished their preflight checklist, including testing all the controls—the rudder, ailerons, elevator, flaps, and spoilers. Phil loved the sounds of the names. The very words were exciting to him.

Uncle Michael snapped his own canopy tight and gave a thumbs-up to the pilot of the tow plane. With the help of the ground crewman, they double-tested the towline release. Then they were ready to go. The ground crewman held the glider level so the craft balanced on its single central wheel, then signaled to the tow pilot that he could proceed. The tow pilot moved the airplane forward, making the towline taut, and then he began to taxi. It didn't take long. In less than a hundred yards, the glider lifted up off the ground, trailing behind the still earthbound tow plane. A few seconds after that, the tow plane was in the air, too.

Without thinking, Phil held his breath. It was as if he didn't want anything to interfere with his concentration on the extraordinary fact that he and Uncle Michael were flying through the sky and in a few minutes they'd be on their own—just the two of them in a beautiful glider with an eighty-four-foot wingspan and nothing but air to hold them up.

"You okay?" Uncle Michael asked over his shoulder.

"Never better," said Phil. And he meant it.

VERONICA LOOKED AT the neat little plane she and Hubert were going to fly in. She couldn't imagine why anybody would fly in a plane without an engine. What did Phil see in gliding around? Then again, she wondered what Phil saw in Stevie Lake. Veronica had much nicer clothes. Perhaps Phil hadn't noticed, any more than he'd noticed her father's bank's very expensive airplane. Well, she could see to it that he did notice. She could see to it that he noticed a lot of things about her, in fact.

"Are you ready now?" Hubert asked.

"Oh, yes," said Veronica.

He opened the small door of the plane and helped her up the cute little set of steps and into a seat. It seemed like a very small seat—much smaller than she was used to in first class on a commercial airliner. But this wasn't a commercial airliner. This was Daddy's bank's plane. And Veronica was going to remind Phil of that.

"Anywhere in particular you want to go, Miss Veronica?" Hubert asked politely.

Veronica looked up into the sky. She could still see the tow plane that was launching Phil and his uncle. In fact, as she watched, she saw the long towline drop from the nose of the glider. The glider found a patch of rising air, circled upward on it, and then floated regally to the east.

"That way," said Veronica, pointing west.

"As you wish," said Hubert.

Of course it's as I wish, Veronica thought. *You work for Daddy. You go where I tell you.*

She smiled, listening to the efficient rumble of the engine as it sparked to life. Wasn't Phil going to be surprised!

12

CAROLE PEERED CAUTIOUSLY around the door of Stevie's room.

"There you are!" Stevie said excitedly, welcoming her friends. "I've been waiting for you for hours! Do you have any idea how lonely it is just sitting here in bed, wondering when my friends are going to arrive?"

Lisa breathed a sigh of relief. Now *that* sounded like the Stevie she knew and loved.

"It's only a few minutes past noon," Lisa reminded her. "And your mother said you just woke up half an hour ago. How lonely can you get in half an hour?"

"Very," Stevie assured her. "But now that you guys are here, I'm not lonely anymore. I'm just happy as can be to see you. Tell me everything that's been happening in the world without me there to make it interesting."

Carole burst into giggles. It felt wonderful to have Stevie back in form. She was relieved, too. Maybe the doctor was right that there had never been anything to worry about.

"Well, nothing very exciting since the sign on Veronica's back and our visit to Mickey Denver's horse ranch," Lisa said. "We did have a mounted Horse Wise meeting this morning, and it was a lot of fun. More fun than usual, in fact. I wonder why."

"There's only one thing that would make Horse Wise more fun than usual, and that is if Veronica isn't there," said Stevie.

"How did you know?" Carole asked her.

"So she wasn't there?" Stevie responded.

"No," said Lisa. "How did you know?"

"It's just logical," Stevie said simply. "Veronica's a damp rag on any party. We all know that."

"Yes, but you seem to know things we all *don't* know," Carole said.

Stevie rolled her eyes up at the ceiling. "Give me a break," she said.

"Give *me* a break," Carole countered. "I mean, you knew about Phil getting thrown by Teddy and you knew Starlight was going to step on my toe and you knew Lisa was calling Deborah Mom."

"Just coincidences," Stevie said.

"But what about your dream with the Point and Laugh sign?" Lisa asked her.

"What about it?" Stevie asked.

"Well, it was like you knew what was going to happen," Lisa said. "Not that I really believe in that supernatural stuff or extrasensory perception or whatever it is; but Stevie, you've got to admit there's something a little bit creepy going on here."

"I don't either," said Stevie. "You guys just have the most fantastic imaginations."

"Right," said Carole. "Like we made it all up?"

"Just like that," said Stevie. "You have made up a lot of things in the past few days, and I have to tell you, it's upsetting to me when you do that."

Lisa realized that Stevie meant what she was saying. She really was getting upset. Her face was reddening, and her eyes were welling with tears. Clearly the idea that she had some sort of superpower disagreed with her.

"Oh, Stevie, we're only kidding," Lisa said. "I guess when you're not around with all your crazy schemes,

Carole and I don't know what to do with our time, so we make stuff up. Don't worry about it. It's just that we miss you. The thing you have to do is concentrate on getting better. In the meantime, we'll try to stay out of trouble, okay?"

Stevie pulled her covers up and slid down into her bed a little. "Thanks, Lisa," she said, smiling weakly. "It confuses me a little bit when I don't feel well. All I really want is to be myself again."

"That's all we want, too," Carole assured her. "And I didn't mean to upset you. I was just being foolish and thoughtless."

"You two are never thoughtless," said Stevie. "You're my best friends."

"Yes, we are," Lisa said.

With that, Stevie's eyelids closed, and in what seemed like a second, she was breathing deeply and evenly. She was asleep.

Lisa tiptoed over to the window on the far side of Stevie's room and motioned for Carole to join her.

"I thought she was okay," Carole whispered.

"Me too," said Lisa. "At first she seemed like the same old Stevie, and then, all of a sudden, Miss Concussion came back. Weird."

"Well, maybe it's not so weird," said Carole. "Maybe

we are making up all these connections between Stevie's strange dreams and the things that are happening. Maybe it is just total coincidence."

"Maybe," said Lisa. "And maybe when she gets tired so fast because of her concussion, she just seems to have an instant personality transplant."

"I want the good old Stevie to come back and *stay* back," Carole said.

"Me too," Lisa said. "As long as we're here, we might as well stay and wait until she wakes up. Then we won't mention any strange coincidences related to anything she might tell us she dreamed about. That should make her feel better, right?"

"Sure, but will it make *us* feel better?" Carole asked.

Lisa smiled at Carole, because that was exactly what was going through her mind. "Probably not," Lisa conceded. "The only thing that will really make us feel better is when Stevie stops behaving like—"

"Phil!"

The cry from Stevie startled Carole and Lisa. They turned to look at Stevie, who was still asleep.

Lisa giggled. "Oh, so she calls out his name in her sleep!"

Carole laughed, too. "I guess when you've got a really nice boyfriend like Phil—"

"Look out!" Stevie cried. There was a terrible look of fear on her face, even though her eyes were closed.

"Oh no, she's having a nightmare," Lisa said.

"We should wake her up," Carole said. She started to walk over to Stevie's bed.

"No," Lisa said, tugging on Carole's sleeve. "I don't think you're supposed to do that. See, if someone's having a nightmare, you've got to let them finish it. Nightmares usually come out all right, but if you cut into the middle of it, the dreamer never knows what the real end is. I read that in a magazine somewhere."

"Pull your feet up!" Stevie cried out. She waved her hands frantically in front of herself, almost as if she were blind and trying to reach out in the blank darkness.

"Are you sure about this?" Carole asked Lisa.

"Well, I'm sure I read it in a magazine," Lisa said. "But I can't guarantee you the person who wrote the article had any idea what they were writing about."

"The trees!" Stevie yelled. With that, she sat bolt upright and her eyes flew open.

"Stevie, are you okay?" Lisa asked.

"What is it, Stevie?" said Carole.

Stevie scratched her head. There was a puzzled look on her face, far from the panicked look she'd had during her dream. "I know this sounds strange," she said, "but Phil is in a tree."

Lisa and Carole exchanged looks. The last thing they wanted to do was to upset Stevie any more than she had been. That was what they'd promised one another.

Lisa smiled warmly at Stevie. "I'm sure he is," she said.

"I bet it's a nice tree, too," said Carole.

"Are you guys nuts?" Stevie asked.

Carole and Lisa were wondering the same thing.

13

PHIL COULD BARELY speak. He and Uncle Michael had been up in the glider for almost an hour, and Phil still couldn't believe it was real. He'd been in many airplanes, but the feeling of a glider was entirely different. It was more as if they were floating than flying. An airplane, Phil realized, vibrated from the engines. The glider rode gently on the wind. Phil could hear the wind everywhere, whistling past the ship and *whish*ing around the wings. It was a natural sound, unlike the clatter and roar of the huge engines airplanes used to stay aloft.

The glider seemed to rise then, and Phil knew Uncle Michael had found another thermal to give them lift.

They banked, turning gently to the right, circling within the thermal. Phil looked down. Four thousand feet below them lay the foothills of Virginia's mountains and the rolling countryside of Willow Creek.

Phil squinted to see if he could get his bearings. He and Uncle Michael had flown east, and he wondered if he could recognize any landmarks. Something in a field below moved. Phil smiled. That wasn't a field, that was a paddock. And that wasn't just something. That was a horse. He studied the land carefully. Could it be?

"Look! There it is!"

"What?" Uncle Michael asked.

"It's Pine Hollow! That's where Stevie rides her horse! She lives nearby, too. Let me see, it's . . ."

Phil tried to envision the walk from Pine Hollow to Stevie's house. There was the main road, and then Stevie's street curving off to one side, and then there were three houses on the left and two, three, four on the right, and then—

"It's Stevie's! That one with the swimming pool, see it?"

"And the three bikes on the front lawn?" Uncle Michael asked.

"There would be four there if Stevie weren't sick now," Phil said.

Uncle Michael laughed. "I used to drop my bike on

the lawn, too," he said. "Now, let's go see how things are doing back at the mountains," he said.

With that, Uncle Michael leveled the craft and began flying back to the west, toward the mountains and Rock Ridge.

"HUBERT!" VERONICA WHINED into the microphone of her headset. "I told you not to let them out of our sight!"

"I thought you wanted to take pictures of clouds and mountains," said the beleaguered pilot, who sat right in front of her. "Clouds are up there and the mountains are—"

"I already took a picture of the dumb mountain," said Veronica. She growled under her breath, making little effort to hide her irritation from Hubert. Hoping Hubert would do something for her to please her father was one thing. Being nice to him while he did it was another. Veronica looked through her camera's viewfinder. To the west, she saw big white fluffy clouds piled on big white fluffy clouds, topped by a deep blue sky. She snapped six pictures in quick succession.

There, that ought to get her to Rome. Now, where was Phil Marsten?

At Veronica's insistence, Hubert brought the airplane to a lower altitude. Veronica didn't see how something without an engine could go very high. And they couldn't have gone far. Veronica thought that Phil and his uncle Michael were totally nuts to fly in that little plane thing without any power, or else they were very brave. It probably took a lot of skill to fly a plane without an engine. Probably it took a lot more skill than dumb Hubert would ever have.

Skill. That was it. Pictures of clouds didn't really meet the contest requirement of pictures that showed somebody doing something that required skill. But a picture of someone flying a glider—now that showed skill. Probably.

If she could take a picture of Phil's uncle Michael, then Phil would be really impressed when she won the contest. It would also be an excellent way for Veronica to point out to Phil that she had a good deal more to offer than Stevie Lake.

Veronica grinned proudly. She loved it when things worked out perfectly for her. And this was going to be perfect. If only Hubert would find them!

"Why don't you call someplace on the radio to find out where they've gone," she said.

"Unfortunately, that will only work if they've called the tower to say where they are," said Hubert.

"So?"

"Yes, Miss," said Hubert. He clicked on the radio obediently. The radio operator in the tower said he had no idea what the flight plan was for the glider.

Veronica was about to suggest that Hubert call another tower when she was spared the trouble. For there, coming from the east, was Uncle Michael's glider!

"There they are!" Veronica squealed. "Don't lose sight of them."

"Yes, Miss," said Hubert.

"NOW, THE RIDE here may be a little rougher than it was out over the valley," said Uncle Michael. "That's because we're near the mountains. We'll get updrafts off the ridges, but we may get rather sudden downdrafts, in which case, we'll need plenty of airspeed to get through them. So we won't get too close to the mountains. However, the care we have to take is worth it because of the views we'll have along the tops of the ridges. This area is spectacular from any angle, but this is my favorite way to see it."

Phil looked to his left through the clear plastic canopy. The view took his breath away. The ridges of the mountaintops rushed past beneath the glider. Their path was so smooth and effortless that it seemed to Phil it must be the mountains themselves that were moving. He smiled at the thought, knowing, of course, that that was ridiculous.

Suddenly there was a roar. The glider bounced downward and jogged to the left toward the mountain ridge, then leveled out.

Unconsciously, Phil grasped the arms of his seat. "What was that?" he asked.

"That was an airplane," said Uncle Michael, gripping the stick tightly. "Some dumb hotdogging pilot who isn't paying any attention to what he's doing—or ought to be doing, anyway. He has no right to pass us on our right when we're so near the mountains!"

Phil saw the tail of the small plane that had whooshed past them. The glider shuddered in the wake of the other craft.

"Jerks!" Phil called out.

"That won't do any good," said Uncle Michael. "But this will." He reached for the radio to warn off the airplane. Phil kept his eye on it nervously.

"He's turning, Uncle Michael," he said.

"Good. They want to get out of here before I report them to the tower."

"No, I mean they're turning around. The plane is coming back this way!"

* * *

112

"NOW THIS TIME, get close enough so I can get a decent picture of the people in the glider!" snapped Veronica.

"But Miss—"

"I'm not going to win this contest with a picture that doesn't show anything." She could imagine Phil's handsome face in her photograph already.

Veronica held the camera up to the window of the small plane and prepared for her winning shot. She could see the glider approaching them rapidly. It was level and soaring smoothly near the mountain ridge. Phil's uncle was in the front seat; Phil was in the back. If she tried to take a picture as they passed them going in the opposite direction, she'd only have a split second. It wouldn't work at all. They would just have to make a big circle and come back and fly parallel to the glider, as they had when they'd passed it the first time. In a few seconds, the planes whizzed past one another too fast for Veronica to take any picture—much less a prizewinning one.

"Turn around and then come along beside them," Veronica instructed Hubert. "Only this time, get closer than before."

"I can't do that, Miss."

There was something serious in his voice. Veronica could tell Hubert didn't like her orders. The last thing she needed was to have him start disobeying her.

"Hubert," she said sternly, "didn't Daddy tell you to take me where I asked you to?"

"I want to, but I have to be concerned for your safety," he said meekly.

"Oh, for goodness' sake, all I'm asking you to do is to reverse direction and catch up to that glider thing again. Planes make turns all the time, Hubert, or are you too new a pilot to know that?"

Hubert opened his mouth to protest, but nothing came out. He began to turn.

Veronica had known he would. She just had to remind him that he had to do what Daddy asked and that he was an inexperienced pilot—perhaps a bit too inexperienced to be working for someone as important as Daddy. Some people just needed to be reminded of things before they would do what they were supposed to do. Hubert would obey her now. She sighed with relief and returned her attention to her camera.

Hubert completed the turn that would bring them parallel to the glider. The mountain was on their left, and soon Phil Marsten would be, too. The plane approached the glider from the rear.

At first all she could see was the delicate silhouette of the glider etched against the white of the clouds in front of them. She snapped a picture. Then, as they neared the glider, Veronica could see the number 13 on the glider's tail. She took a picture of that, too. She wanted to win the contest with a picture of Phil and his uncle; but if they didn't come out, she had to have something else.

"Closer!" she called out to Hubert. Obediently, he edged to the left. Veronica could feel her pulse quicken with excitement. She hoped they'd be close enough for Phil to look and to realize just whom he was seeing in the plane. She'd smile and wave. He'd be so impressed!

It was going to be a great picture, too. They weren't that far from the background of the craggy mountain. The picture would have sky, mountain, glider, and, if she was lucky, a grinning Phil Marsten.

They drew parallel to the glider. The plane was going much faster than the glider, so she didn't have much time.

Click. Whir. Click. Whir. The tail. The fuselage. Now the angle was right to catch the dramatic stretch of the glider's long wings. The clear plastic hood was visible. And there was the back of Phil's head. *Click. Whir.* Veronica knew she was getting the photographs of a lifetime.

"Closer!" she said.

Hubert didn't answer. Then, suddenly and without

warning, the plane hit a gust and seemed to bounce over to the left, much closer to the glider. They weren't just passing the glider, they were cutting right in front of it! The glider made a sudden and dramatic turn toward the mountain. *Click. Whir.* It was elegant and beautiful! She even got a picture of the glider as it slid off to the left.

"Fabulous!" said Veronica, snapping pictures as fast as she could. She hadn't had time to wave at Phil, but both Phil and his uncle were waving at her. "Rome, here I come!" she declared.

"Hold on!" Hubert cried out.

The plane jerked and rattled. Hubert wrestled with the controls. "We'll get out of this!" he yelled.

"Out of what?" Veronica asked.

Hubert didn't answer. He pulled at the stick and made a sharp banking turn upward and to the right. When Veronica looked straight ahead, she saw why. They were headed straight into the mountain!

"Hubert!" she screamed.

The plane's nose lifted, and the mountain seemed to fall away. Ahead was blue sky and then the level green land of the valley. They were out of danger.

"What do you think you were doing back there, Hubert?" Veronica demanded.

"Just what Daddy wanted," he answered politely.

* * *

116

THE GLIDER SHOOK violently in the abrupt turn. Phil watched in horror as Uncle Michael skillfully pulled his craft out of the path of the airplane. The glider's right wing missed the plane's tail by inches! That disaster was averted, but there was another one just ahead. They were headed right into the mountain!

Suddenly it was as if the glider stopped. They'd lost their forward speed in the emergency turn.

"We've stalled!" Uncle Michael said.

Phil could feel the glider losing altitude. It was almost as if it were being sucked downward. The glider shuddered in the turbulent currents that played over the mountaintops.

"It's a sink!" Uncle Michael called out.

Phil watched Uncle Michael check his instruments. Uncle Michael was an experienced pilot. He knew what to do, and he wasn't going to be helped by any panic from the backseat. Phil held on grimly. The scene flashed through his mind again. That little plane had been passing them on the outside. When an air current had pushed the plane into their path, Uncle Michael was forced to move closer to the mountain crest. They'd stalled, and then turbulence over the crest had pulled them closer still. Now they were in a downdraft—a sink—and they were dropping by the second. If they didn't find lift, they were going to crash!

The mountain loomed larger at every second. Uncle Michael held the stick firmly, looking for a place to land. All Phil could see were trees and rocky crags.

"Pull your feet up, cover your face!" Uncle Michael yelled.

Phil did it. He felt a violent jerk and heard a sickening sound. A moan and a snap. Their right wing was torn off in an instant.

It seemed like an eternity of thunderous noises and wrenching jerks as the glider propelled itself through the treetops.

And then there was silence.

Phil could feel a motion, ever so slight. At first he thought he was imagining it. He raised his head and looked out through the canopy. All he could see were treetops and sky. The earth was still below them— twenty-five feet below them. The glider had come to rest in a tree.

"Uncle Michael?" Phil asked. There was a long silence. "Are you all right?"

The only response he got was a groan.

"SHE'S BEEN ASLEEP for over an hour now," Carole whispered to Lisa.

"And she hasn't been talking anymore."

Carole looked over at Stevie, who was sleeping restfully.

The door of Stevie's room opened a crack. Mrs. Lake peeked in and smiled to see her daughter sleeping so well.

"Come on down to the kitchen and have a snack," she invited Lisa and Carole. The girls got up and followed her. They would be glad to talk without worrying about disturbing Stevie. As soon as they got into the kitchen, they sensed that there was something new to worry about. There was a dark look of concern on Mrs. Lake's face.

"What is it?" Lisa asked.

"It shows, doesn't it? I tried to hide it, but the only one in the family who can keep a secret is Stevie."

"What's the matter?" Carole asked.

Mrs. Lake sat down at the table. The girls joined her. "I had a call from Phil's mother," she said. "He and his uncle are late getting back to the airport."

"Oh, I bet they're just having fun flying around," said Lisa. "I read some things about gliding, and if you get the right conditions, you can stay up for hours!"

"Well, they've been up for hours already," said Mrs. Lake. "And they're not answering radio calls."

Lisa got a hard feeling in the pit of her stomach.

"Maybe they just had the thing turned off?" Carole suggested optimistically.

Lisa shook her head. "No," she said. "They would always have the radio on so they could get calls when they're in the air."

"Maybe it's just broken?" Carole tried again.

"Maybe," said Mrs. Lake.

Lisa thought of their friend sleeping soundly upstairs. She shuddered, recalling Stevie's nightmare. Was it a nightmare? Was it the truth? She looked over at Carole.

"Don't even say it," said Carole.

"What?" Mrs. Lake asked.

"Nothing," said Lisa. She hoped it was nothing. She didn't want to believe that Stevie could actually have some sort of second sight. The idea that she could know what had happened or was going to happen was too scary. "Really, nothing," she assured Mrs. Lake.

Mrs. Lake shrugged. "Well, I don't know what's happened to Phil, but I do know that Stevie hasn't been herself lately and I don't want to worry her with this business. You won't say anything, will you? Not until we know exactly what's going on, anyway. Promise?"

Both Lisa and Carole promised. There was no reason to get Stevie upset when nobody knew what there was —or wasn't—to get upset about. They'd wait.

"UNCLE MICHAEL?" PHIL REPEATED. "Are you okay?"

"Sort of," Uncle Michael finally answered from the front seat of the glider. "My ankle hurts an awful lot. I'm afraid it's broken. What about you?"

Phil did a quick inventory of himself. He wiggled his feet and his legs as much as he could in the confines of the cramped rear seat. No problem. His arms were okay, too. His head hurt a little. He reached up and felt a swelling on his forehead where it had bumped into his canopy.

"Just an egg on my head," he said.

"Good. That's really good," said Uncle Michael.

"What do we do next?" Phil asked.

"We get help," said Uncle Michael. He picked up the radio microphone and flipped a switch. There was no reassuring hiss. He tried again. Nothing. He fiddled with a few of the dials and clicked some buttons. Nothing.

"I'm afraid we lost the radio," said Uncle Michael. "We're on our own until somebody comes to find us."

"Well, surely the dopey pilot of that airplane will report what happened," said Phil.

"A pilot that dopey might not have the sense to do that. He might not even have the sense to realize what happened. Also, he had his own problems to cope with. The last I saw of that plane, he was in almost as much trouble as we were."

"And how much trouble are we in now?" Phil asked.

"Depends on how you feel about living in a tree house," said Uncle Michael.

Phil chuckled. If they could laugh, they could survive. At least he hoped that was true.

Phil assessed the situation for himself. The glider seemed to be securely lodged in the tree branches. Uncle Michael's broken ankle would make it impossible for him to get out of the glider, much less climb down the tree.

Phil unlatched the plastic canopy over his head. It stuck for a second and then flipped up. At least one thing on the glider still worked. He peered out over the edge of the glider's fuselage. It was lodged in the V of a split tree trunk. One wing had broken off. The other rested on a broad branch, holding the glider level. That was the good news. The bad news was that they were more than twenty feet off the ground, and there was no way Uncle Michael could make it down.

Phil pulled himself out of his seat and gingerly climbed onto a branch. It was secure. He sighed with relief.

From there he could reach Uncle Michael and all the emergency equipment in the glider. There was a lot of work to be done. Phil looked at his watch. It was six o'clock. There were only a couple of hours of light left. With luck, a rescue plane would find them before night-fall. Without luck, they'd spend this night, and perhaps longer, waiting for help.

Phil took out the first aid kit. There was a bandage that Uncle Michael could use to wrap his ankle.

"I'm afraid it's not necessary," said Uncle Michael. "I'm wearing a boot that gives it some support, but the fact is I can't move it in any direction without excruciating pain, so there's no need to keep it secure right now. It's secure without any help."

123

Phil tucked the bandage into his pocket. He knew they'd need it when the time came to move Uncle Michael—even though he didn't have any idea how he would be able to do that.

There was also a small supply of a painkiller.

"Morphine," Uncle Michael explained. "I don't need it now. I may need it badly later. Hold on to it because we've only got the one dose."

The realization that they might be stuck on the mountain long enough to need more than one dose of morphine made Phil shiver. He put the medicine in the pocket with the bandage.

"If you can get down to the ground, you should set up a campsite for yourself," said Uncle Michael. "I'm stuck up here, but if you can light a fire in an open area, that'll give the rescuers something to spot, especially at night. Here, take my Swiss Army knife. It might come in handy." Phil put that in his pocket, too.

Phil checked the water and food supply. Was it only a few hours ago that he had laughed at Uncle Michael for bringing water and granola bars? He gave Uncle Michael a drink of water and left the canteen with him. Phil was pretty sure he'd find a source of water in the mountain woods below. He took three of the six granola bars, the small tool kit, and a book of matches.

"Holler if you need anything!" he said as cheerfully as

he could manage, and then picked his way down the tree.

When Phil reached the ground and looked up, he felt a pang of despair. The trees were high and thick. The glider had landed in the middle of a tree. It was masked from above by the long shady branches of the tall pine. The glider loomed over his head, making a dark shadow in the fading sunlight.

He knew he could start a fire right near the plane, but the overhead growth was so dense that the blaze might not be seen from the sky. Worse, it might start a forest fire. That would bring rescuers, but they would likely arrive too late. He had to find an open space.

Phil set out. The woods were thick, and the ground was covered with a dense undergrowth of bushes and vines. Tall trees that had fallen over the years criss-crossed the steep forest floor with their trunks. It was slow going.

Phil couldn't see what lay ahead. Everywhere he looked, all he could see was forest. Instead of knowing where he was going, it would be essential for him to know where he'd been. The last thing he wanted was to forget where the glider and Uncle Michael were. He opened the largest blade of the pocket knife and used it to make blazes on the trees of his trail so he could follow them back to the glider.

After more than an hour of trekking, he came to an open space. It was a large, craggy rock outcropping that clung to the side of the mountain and overlooked the valley. Phil recognized it as Rock Ridge, which he'd seen from the airport and the sky. What he hadn't known from those distances was how vast the open rocky area was. Night was starting to fall, and Phil could see a few lights in the distance—perhaps five miles across the open valley.

"Well, if I can see their lights, they'll be able to see mine," he said. His voice sounded loud in the quiet twilight.

Using the flashlight from the tool kit, Phil found some dry branches, twigs, and leaves. It was enough to start a meager fire. As soon as he had a small flame going, he added more dry branches. It wasn't much of a fire, but it would do for now. Quickly he gathered more wood from the forest floor and kept it near the little fire. He sat down next to it and ate his first granola bar. It tasted dry and uninteresting—not nearly as good as it would have been if he had had a glass of water to go with it, or better yet, a soda. Maybe some juice. It would be even nicer if he had a hamburger to go with it—one with a slice of cheese and some bacon. Oh, and some fries, too.

Within a few minutes, Phil had worked himself up an imaginary dinner of huge proportions, delicious, juicy, and totally unavailable. He took the last bite of his granola bar and chewed slowly. The hamburger would have to wait.

Phil had brought his parachute along, wondering if it might come in handy. It became a pillow, insulating him against the ridged rocks. Phil put his head back and looked up at the stars—so many, so far away, so alone, just like Phil.

He closed his eyes. The tension, worry, and exhaustion of the day overtook him. Within a minute, he was asleep. Then he was dreaming. He dreamed of food and a comfortable bed. He dreamed that he was at home, that nothing bad had ever happened to him. Then he dreamed that he was taking a shower, a cold one, noisy and unpleasant. There was a roar and a bright light and the water kept pelting at him. He reached for the spigot and twisted frantically, but the flow didn't stop.

Phil woke up from his nightmare—only to find it wasn't a nightmare. It was reality. Although the sky had been clear when he had dozed off, now it was covered with clouds. He was in the middle of a fierce rainstorm, complete with lightning. The little fire was drenched and doused.

A jagged bolt of lightning raced through the sky. Phil knew he was in danger of getting struck, standing alone on the rocky outcrop. He had to get away from there.

Then he remembered Uncle Michael. How was he doing in the tree in the rain?

Phil grabbed the remains of his food and his matches and headed back into the woods. He left the parachute because it was heavy with water from the rain. He searched his memory, hoping he would be able to find the blazes he'd made on the trees so he could return to the crash site in the dark. In the cold. In the rain.

THE PHONE NEXT TO Lisa's bed rang. She and Carole both jumped at the same second, and Lisa knew that they both had exactly the same thought. Phil. They'd found him. Everything was okay. They didn't have to worry anymore.

But that wasn't it.

"Hi, Lisa? It's Stevie. Why did you guys leave?"

Lisa clutched the telephone hard. She'd known Stevie was going to call her. What she hadn't known was what she would say. On the other hand, this was a fairly straightforward question. She could answer it.

"Carole and I stayed with you for a while, but you

were sound asleep, and it's like you really need the sleep, so we left right before dinner."

"Oh, I guess I woke up a little while after that. Mom gave me some soup. I guess she thinks I'm really sick or something. She only ever gives me soup when she thinks that. I guess I've been a little weird lately, huh?"

"A little," Lisa admitted. "But the doctor says you're getting better."

"If he thinks that, he ought to take a look at my dreams!" said Stevie.

"What do you mean by that?" Lisa asked.

"It was another horse dream," Stevie said. "And this time it was about a blind horse. Maybe I just dreamt that because you told me about that mare you looked at. Blondie, right?"

"Uh, right," said Lisa. "Uh, wait a sec. Carole is here. She's spending the night. Let me get her to pick up an extension, okay?"

Lisa covered the phone and whispered to Carole that Stevie had had another dream. "You've got to hear it, too."

Carole ran and picked up the cordless phone from the hall and brought it back into Lisa's room. They listened together.

"I'm here, Stevie," Carole said brightly.

130

"Are you okay?" Stevie asked immediately. "You sound funny."

"I'm fine," Carole said, trying to sound as normal as possible. These days it wasn't easy sounding normal around Stevie.

"Okay, so here's what happened in my dream. This horse is struggling someplace."

"Like it's sick or something?"

"Oh, no," said Stevie. "Not at all. She's struggling because she has to climb something. It's really tough going. She's climbing a mountain maybe. There are rocks everywhere, but she doesn't see them. All she can see is that she's got to get there. Somehow, she knows it's really important."

"What is?" Lisa asked.

"Whatever it is," said Stevie. "I don't know. I mean, nobody's told me what's important. I just know the horse knows."

"Wow," said Carole. "That's an exciting dream."

"I think I should start writing these things down," said Stevie. "These dreams I've been having are good ones. Don't you think it would make a good story? Nobody would believe it, of course. But dreams are dreams."

"That's right," Lisa said quickly. "Dreams *are* dreams. These are dreams, aren't they?"

"That's what I said, didn't I?" Stevie asked. There was

an edge to her voice, and Lisa knew she was pushing a little too hard. She didn't want to upset Stevie, especially when there was so much she didn't want to have to explain.

"Of course," Lisa said.

"I sure wish I could be with you guys tonight. I'm tired of being sick. I'm even tired of being tired. I want to be well. I want to stop having strange dreams. Know what I think this is all about?"

"What?" Carole asked.

"I think my mind is so bored with being in bed all the time that it keeps on making up strange stuff."

"I'm sure you're right," said Carole, but she wasn't sure at all.

"Well, to keep me from having wild dreams, you guys have to tell me everything you're doing. What are your plans for tomorrow?"

"Oh, we'll just go to Pine Hollow and hang around," Carole said. "We'll check on Belle for you."

"Thanks," Stevie said. "And tell her I will get better and I will ride her really soon, okay?"

"Deal," Carole said.

"And we'll stop by tomorrow, too," said Lisa. "Probably late in the day."

"Phil said he'd come by, too," said Stevie. "Have you talked with him?"

132

"Um, no, not, er, today," said Lisa.

"Of course you haven't talked with him today," Stevie said, almost snapping. "He's been up in that glider with his uncle. The two of them have been having a wonderful time, and Phil hasn't even had the consideration to give me a call to let me know that he's all right. I have half a mind to call him right now."

"Oh, I wouldn't do that," Lisa said quickly.

"Why not?" Stevie asked.

"Well, it's—I mean, probably if they were flying all day—um . . ."

"It's pretty late," Carole said. "I bet those two were so tired they just fell asleep as soon as they got home."

"You're probably right," said Stevie. "I'll call him in the morning."

"Um, Stevie?" Carole began.

"No, I won't," Stevie said, correcting herself. "I don't need to chase him down. If he wants to talk to me, his friend who is sick in bed, well, then he can just give me a call. I'm certainly not going to call him!"

"Good idea," said Lisa.

"Good night," Stevie said, and then she hung up.

"Whew," said Carole.

"Definitely," agreed Lisa.

16

LISA AND CAROLE arose before dawn the next morning. They wanted to get to Pine Hollow early to look after Belle for Stevie and to take an early trail ride. Later in the day, the woods around Pine Hollow would be filled with other riders, a lot of them inexperienced. At daybreak they'd have the place to themselves.

"I think dawn is my favorite time of day to ride," said Lisa, vigorously brushing Belle's coat.

"I think my favorite time is any time," said Carole.

Lisa laughed. That was just like Carole. Even though they were all horse-crazy, Carole was probably the horse-craziest of them all. She brought Belle some grain and filled her hayrack.

"Don't worry, old girl," Lisa said, patting the horse's smooth nose and rubbing her cheek just where she liked it best. "Stevie will be back here in no time. She'll be riding you again, and she'll get you back to working on jumps so she can beat Phil—"

Lisa stopped suddenly, realizing what she'd said. For a moment, she'd forgotten about Phil. There had been no call last night. None this morning. Phil and his uncle were still missing. She swallowed hard.

"Oh, they'll find them," said Carole. "They can't have gone far, and you're the one who was telling me how safe gliders are. They couldn't search last night because of the dark and the rain. But the sun's out today. There will be helicopters and planes all over the place. They'll find them and they'll be okay."

"But they were flying right near Mickey Denver's ranch. You remember what the terrain looks like over there—the mountains are rocky and they looked dangerous to me."

Carole was quiet for a moment. She dropped Belle's brush into her grooming bucket and unclipped the crossties. Lisa patted Belle as Carole shooed her into the stall, and then Lisa clipped the lock shut.

"I wish there were something we could do," said Carole.

"What could we do? I mean, shouldn't rescuing be left to professionals?" Lisa asked. "We don't even know where to begin."

"Or how," Carole said.

"It would be a real challenge as a Saddle Club project," said Lisa.

"For something this difficult, we'd have to have Stevie's help," Carole agreed.

"We'd have to have more help than that," Lisa said glumly.

In the end, they decided there really wasn't much they could do except hope that everything would turn out okay.

"Let's go on our trail ride. Maybe when we get back, Stevie's mother will already have called Mrs. Reg to tell us that everything's fine," Lisa suggested.

"Good idea," Carole said.

They saddled up and left the Pine Hollow paddocks behind. The woods were magically quiet at that early-morning hour. The leaves were still damp with rain from the night before. Lisa was enjoying the ride until the thought occurred to her that Phil and his uncle might be stranded in the woods somewhere. They might have been caught in last night's downpour. They might be lost and scared . . . or worse.

Carole seemed to be thinking the same thing.

"Let's go back," she said to Lisa. "This isn't working."

"I bet Mrs. Lake has called already," said Lisa.

"Are you starting to read minds, too?" Carole asked.

"I hope not," Lisa told her honestly. "I don't think I'd like to know what's going to happen—unless it's all good news."

"Me neither," Carole agreed, turning Starlight around.

It only took them fifteen minutes to get back to Pine Hollow, even walking their horses for the last quarter mile. Mrs. Reg was there, but she didn't have any news for them.

"Who's going to call you at this hour of the morning?" she asked.

Carole and Lisa explained about Phil and his uncle.

"Oh dear," said Mrs. Reg. She scratched her head thoughtfully. "You know, there was a horse we had here once—used to run away all the time. At first my Max—the one you girls call Max the Second"—that was Max's father—"he'd ride all over the place just looking for that fellow. Then he stopped."

Carole and Lisa waited a second until they realized

that Mrs. Reg was done with her story. She often told stories, and they often ended abruptly. They didn't usually end this abruptly, though.

"So what happened?" Lisa asked.

"Did he just disappear?" asked Carole.

"Of course not," said Mrs. Reg. "He was a valuable horse. But I can't stand here telling you girls stories all day long. I've got to get to work, and from the looks of your horses, you've got some work to do, too. Do you think Starlight and Prancer want to wait all morning for their breakfast?" With that, she turned and walked into her office.

Carole and Lisa looked at one another, shrugged, and dismounted. Sometimes it took a few minutes to figure out what Mrs. Reg's stories were about. Sometimes they never figured them out.

This time it took exactly as long as it took Lisa to remove Prancer's tack.

"Got it!" she announced over the stable wall.

"Me too," Carole said. "Max stopped riding all over the place to find the horse because the horse always came back on his own, whether they looked for him or not."

"That's what I think, too," Lisa agreed. She hoped that meant that Phil and his uncle would find their way to safety, with or without the help of The Saddle Club.

She hefted Prancer's saddle and bridle with her linked arms and carried them to the tack room. The door was partly closed. Lisa opened it wider by shoving it gently with her hip.

"Oomph!" came a distraught voice on the other side.

"I'm sorry," Lisa said, edging into the room. But she wished she could take back her words as soon as she saw to whom she had apologized. It was Veronica diAngelo, who was examining her horse's tack.

"Well, you should be," Veronica said. Lisa thought that was a pretty rude way to accept an apology, but she considered the source and decided not to make any more of it. "I mean, nothing seems to go right around here. First Red has done a careless job with my tack, and now you barge in here like you own the place."

Lisa swallowed what she really wanted to say. She'd learned long ago that it didn't make any difference what one said to Veronica.

"Gee, Veronica, we sure missed you yesterday."

"Did you?" Veronica asked, arching her eyebrows in a way Lisa hoped she'd never do herself. "Well, I had something else I had to do."

"What was that?" Lisa asked. She was immediately sorry. Asking Veronica a question like that always led up to a long boring story about how wonderful Veronica was. This time was no exception.

"Well, I had another photo session for that contest that will take me to Rome."

"Oh, you mean you didn't think the photographs of Stevie's accident were dramatic enough?" Lisa asked.

"Not really," Veronica said, completely missing Lisa's sarcasm. "But these are. I know I've got a winner. In fact, last evening, I made Mother take me to the mall to buy an Italian phrase book. I have to be able to say, 'How much is that in dollars?' and 'Do you take credit cards?' I had my photographs developed right away. Would you like to see them?"

Lisa didn't want to let Veronica trap her in one of her "admire me" conversations, but she couldn't resist. She loved photography and was always curious to see other people's work. She also wanted to know what Veronica thought was a prizewinning photograph.

"Sure, Veronica, why not?" she said. She put Prancer's saddle on its rack and followed Veronica to the locker area. Carole was there, taking off her boots. She seemed surprised when she saw Lisa and Veronica together, but she understood when Lisa explained that it had to do with photographs. She was curious about Veronica's certain victory in the photo contest, too. She pulled on her sneakers and joined Lisa by Veronica's cubby.

Veronica pulled an envelope out of her designer handbag and handed it to Lisa. "See for yourself," she said. "Personally, I think there are five or six pictures there that would win any contest, anywhere, but I'm not sure which is the very best of them. Lisa, didn't you take some sort of photography class sometime? You might be able to help me choose . . ."

Lisa closed her ears to Veronica's prattle. She didn't need a guided tour. The photographs had to speak for themselves. She pulled the prints out of the envelope.

". . . so I had Daddy's pilot take me up. You can't imagine how hard it was to make him understand that these couldn't be just any old photographs . . ."

The first photograph was simply blue. It took Lisa a moment to realize she was looking at a photograph of sky. She handed it to Carole.

". . . so I told him in no uncertain terms exactly what he had to do. You know how these people are . . ."

The second photograph was of sky and clouds. It was pretty, but it didn't seem very special until Lisa realized that it was taken very close to the clouds.

". . . and you can't imagine how awful it was to bounce around in that thing. If I ever have my own plane—and I'm sure I will—it's going to be larger so I'll have a smoother ride . . ."

The next photograph was of a mountainside. Lisa looked at it twice before she recognized it.

"Rock Ridge," she said, handing the photograph to Carole.

"Well, of course it's Rock Ridge," said Veronica. "It was right near the airport. We never did go far away, you know. That silly man . . ."

The next photograph had something else in it. At first all Lisa saw was the vague outline of a shadow against the cloud. The photograph was blurred.

". . . well, we hit some sort of air pocket or something there. It was terribly bouncy the whole time. You can't imagine . . ."

"Look, Carole, it's a glider!" said Lisa. Carole looked over her shoulder. Lisa shifted that photograph to the back of the pile and looked at the next one. It was of the glider's tail.

"Is that . . . ?" Carole asked. The girls squinted to make out the marking on the tail of the glider. Lisa switched to the next picture.

"Number thirteen!"

"It's Phil's uncle's glider!" Carole said.

Veronica preened. "Yes, it is," she said. "Do you think Phil will be pleased?"

Lisa was so stunned she couldn't answer the question. She looked at the next few photographs. She saw that the plane had gotten much closer to the glider, and then there was a picture where both of the people in the glider had their hands up.

"They're waving at me!" Veronica announced proudly. "Of course, then that silly Hubert said we just had to go home. He spent a whole lot of time making a fancy turn. I think the man was just trying to make me sick to my stomach. I told Daddy all about it as soon as I got home and he said he'd give Hubert a piece of his mind. It's no more than he deserves . . ."

Lisa examined that picture carefully. There was something very odd about the way they were waving. But it wasn't until she looked at the next picture that she realized what it was.

In the next photograph, the glider was banking extremely sharply to the left and was aiming down!

"Carole!" Lisa said. "This is it! This is what happened!"

There were no more photographs.

"Well, which one of the pictures do you think is the winner?" Veronica demanded.

"We've got to do something," said Carole.

"Right away," Lisa agreed.

Lisa handed the whole stack of pictures to Veronica. There was no time to waste telling her what she'd done. There was never any point in trying to tell Veronica anything.

17

"WAIT A MINUTE! What are we going to do?" Carole called to Lisa as she trailed out of the locker area after her.

"We've got to get to a phone!" Lisa said. "We have to call the airport." She darted into Mrs. Reg's office, where there was a phone on the desk. But the phone was being used at the moment. Deborah was just hanging up.

"Oh, just who I was looking for," she began, but she stopped when she saw the looks on Lisa's and Carole's faces. "What's the matter?"

Lisa explained what had happened.

"You mean Phil and his uncle are missing?"

"Right, and Veronica had pictures—they must have crashed. We know right where they are! Or at least where they were last seen!" said Lisa.

"It's next to Rock Ridge," Carole said. "We saw it in the photographs. Somebody's got to be told."

It only took Deborah a few seconds to get the number for the airport and to relay the information. Deborah listened carefully for a few minutes and then thanked the woman and hung up.

"She talked over the radio to the pilot of the rescue plane, and he's going to go look for them in that area again now. I guess—well, we'll see."

"What?" Lisa asked. There was more. She knew it. There was something Deborah didn't want to say.

"Phil's our friend. Please tell us," Lisa begged.

"Maybe it's nothing. We shouldn't worry unnecessarily, but—well—the woman said she knew the area. It's very dense woods. It's hard to see in there, and it's even harder to rescue," Deborah said.

"Those mountains didn't look that difficult," Carole said. "Remember we saw the place when we were at Mickey Denver's ranch? I mean, we've been to the Rockies: That's no place for a rescue. This ought to be easy."

Deborah nodded. "It ought to be, but apparently it's not. After the plane has located them, it's going to be

146

extremely difficult to get rescue vehicles into the woods, because the only access to the mountains is by narrow trails."

"Too narrow for trucks?" Lisa asked, realizing what that might mean.

"That's what the woman said," Deborah told the girls.

"But not too narrow for, say, a horse?" asked Carole.

"No, of course not, but the trails are treacherous. You'd have a devil of a time convincing a horse to climb up the rocky path the woman at the airport was describing."

Lisa looked over at her friend. "Are you thinking what I think you're thinking?" she asked her friend.

"I think I am," said Carole.

"What's going on here?" Deborah asked.

"It's Stevie," Lisa explained.

"What's Stevie got to do with this?"

"It's not exactly *Stevie*," said Carole. "It's just what we've come to think of as *Stevian* thinking. When you hang around that girl long enough, you start to see the world the way she does."

"And exactly how would she see this particular problem?" Deborah asked.

"She'd see it as a problem that can be solved by a blind horse," Lisa said.

147

"You've got to be kidding!" Deborah said. "How do you fig—"

"Come on, Deborah," Carole cut in. "I don't think there's a second to waste. Let's go. We'll explain on the way."

Deborah obediently grabbed her wallet and her keys and ran after the girls to her car. She turned the key in the ignition and shifted the car into gear. Suddenly she stopped and looked at her passengers.

"Where are we going?" she asked.

"To Mickey Denver's, of course!" Lisa said. "We need a blind horse to go on a treacherous rescue mission."

"Oh," said Deborah. "I think I see now. But what if he's already sold Blondie to another buyer?" Deborah asked.

"No way!" said Carole. "Who's going to buy a blind horse?"

"Oh, right," said Deborah. She pulled a cellular phone out of her glove compartment. Deborah hesitated for a second. "You know," she said to Carole and Lisa, "I think I know a way to rescue two birds with one stone. You can ride Blondie to Rock Ridge, *and* I can still write my investigative story for the paper. Let's see if this works." She punched in the number for Mickey Denver.

Mr. Denver was away, but his stable manager was there and had been told that Mrs. Hale and her daughter might be back for another look at Blondie. Sure, he'd have her saddled up for the girl to ride and they could come any time. Western Saddle? No problem. And a rope, too? What does your daughter want to do, practice rounding up cattle? Heh. Heh. Oh, well, of course, anything she wants, Mrs. Hale. Fifteen minutes? Blondie will be ready for your little girl then, Mrs. Hale. Why, in that time, I can have her coat gleaming—okay, fine, I'll see you then.

"Remember," Deborah said, snapping her phone closed. "He'll never let you take the horse out of the paddock if he suspects any funny business."

"Time for a star performance," Lisa said. "That'll be my job."

"Then I'm going to specialize in rescue tactics," said Carole.

Lisa wrestled briefly with her conscience, realizing that while her plan with Carole was a good one and an important one and might be the best way to reach Phil and his uncle, what they were proposing to do was an unauthorized "borrowing" of a horse. The words *false pretenses* floated through her mind more than once.

"Oh, stop thinking too hard," said Carole, reading her friend's mind. "Don't forget, this is a man who was willing to sell us a horse without mentioning the fact that the poor creature is totally blind!"

149

Lisa sighed with relief. Carole was absolutely right.

The stable manager at the Denver ranch was named Moe. He turned out to be as dull as Mr. Denver was sharp. Moe never sensed that anything foul was afoot, even when Lisa and Carole both climbed up into the saddle. Lisa thought that would be a giveaway, but he just smiled sweetly.

"She's a nice horse, that Blondie," he said as he handed the reins trustingly to Lisa. "Now don't take her too far, will you?"

Lisa glanced across the valley and up to the mountains at the valley's end. She could see the craggy overhang of Rock Ridge clearly.

"Don't worry," she assured Moe. "We'll be in sight."

"Good," he said. "And we'll be watching you the whole time."

"Of course," said Lisa. She gave Blondie a little kick. The horse began going forward obediently at a pleasant plodding walk.

As Lisa and Carole rode away, they could hear Deborah begin to do her part.

"Excuse me, but do you think I might use the bathroom?" she asked.

"Oh, sure, Mrs. Hale," said the polite stable manager.

"Can you show me where it is, Moe?"

"Sure, Mrs. Hale."

Carole looked back over her shoulder and watched the two adults disappear into the barn.

"They're gone," she told Lisa.

Lisa nudged Blondie with her heels. The horse shifted into an obedient trot. In a minute they reached the gate in the paddock. Carole opened it with her riding crop and then swung it closed behind them.

"How long do you think Deborah can keep Moe from seeing we've gone?" Carole asked.

"She's a pro," Lisa assured her. "After the bathroom comes the telephone, and then she's going to need a drink of water."

"Then she's supposed to ask him to give her a tour of the barn 'where Blondie lives,'" Carole said, smirking. They'd spent most of their drive to Rock Ridge making suggestions to Deborah about how she could distract the stable manager.

"I think the truly inspired suggestion was mine," Carole said to Lisa.

"Oh, right, the part where Deborah is supposed to ask Moe if he can show her how to muck out a stall?" Lisa said, grinning in spite of their serious mission. "If I've judged that man right, he'll be overseeing Deborah while she mucks out every stall in Mickey Denver's barn!"

"She only has to do it long enough to let us get out of

sight," said Carole. "And if you can get Blondie up to a canter, we should manage to disappear in about five minutes. That's less than one good mucking! Look! There's the trail!" she said.

Carole held Lisa's waist while Lisa touched Blondie's belly behind her girth. Blondie obediently broke into a smooth canter toward the opening in the woods. The trail would take them up the mountain that loomed in the distance.

The girls held on and watched carefully. Blondie was so well trained that she did exactly what she was told with faith that her riders weren't going to get her into trouble. Lisa and Carole were accustomed to riding a horse that could spot an obstacle and get around or over it without help. But Lisa had to do all the thinking for Blondie.

The first problem was a gopher hole. Lisa moved the reins ever so slightly to the left; Blondie responded immediately, shifting to the left. Then she returned to the original direction at Lisa's instruction.

"You know, I'm beginning to think this magnificent horse is everything Mickey Denver said she was."

"If I remember correctly, the only thing he promised us was a silky mane."

"Right," said Lisa. "And Blondie's got a lot more than that to offer."

"Here comes a tree!" Carole said.

Quickly, Lisa got Blondie to swerve to the right. She decided then that she couldn't afford to chat with Carole. If she talked, she'd run the risk of forgetting to be Blondie's eyes while the horse was their feet.

A few minutes later they entered the woods at the base of the steep hill that led to Rock Ridge.

"This definitely looks like a path," Carole said. "We're on our way!"

Lisa drew Blondie to a walk. There would be no more cantering, or even trotting, now that they were in the woods. "This is definitely a path," Lisa agreed. "I just hope it's the right one."

Carole hoped so, too. There was no room for error. It simply *had* to be the right one.

The path wound through the dense forest. It sloped gently upward, indicating to the girls that they were going the right way. Carole held on and crossed her fingers. She suspected Lisa would be doing the same thing, except it might interfere with the way she handled the reins—and to Blondie, all signals were significant.

The horse's head rose and dropped with each footstep. She moved forward, exactly as instructed.

"There's a tree fallen down ahead," Lisa said.

"Go around it," Carole told her.

"I can't," Lisa said, bringing Blondie to a halt. "There's no room to leave the path."

"Then we have to go over it," Carole said. She slid off Blondie's back and considered the possibilities.

There was only one. They had to go on ahead. Carole took a gentle grip on the reins near the bit.

"Come on, girl," she said, clucking her tongue encouragingly. "You can do this."

Blondie moved forward obediently. When they reached the fallen tree, Carole realized that she was going to have to let Blondie understand exactly how high and wide the fallen tree was.

She brought the horse to a halt immediately in front of the trunk. She slid her hand down Blondie's right front leg as if she wanted to clean her shoe. The mare lifted her foot. Carole took it firmly in her hand and placed it on the top of the tree trunk. Then, tugging gently, she moved it forward to the far side of the trunk. At first Blondie seemed a little confused. She pulled her foot back. Carole picked it up again and repeated her lesson, clucking her tongue encouragingly.

"She's going to get it. I know she is," Lisa said, more hopeful than sure.

"You bet she is," Carole said with confidence. She put her riding crop gently against the back of Blondie's other foreleg, reminding her that forward was the direction to

154

go. The horse stepped forward with her left hind leg. Her left foreleg went over the tree trunk, and the two hind legs followed in rapid succession.

"Good girl!" Carole declared triumphantly as she climbed back up behind Lisa.

They continued their ascent.

The trail wasn't easy or smooth. Carole had to get off two more times to help Blondie over other obstacles. Another time, she had to get the horse to duck under a low overhanging branch. Each time, Blondie simply did what she was told, as soon as she understood what was needed.

"You know what, Carole?" Lisa asked.

"What?"

"I'm beginning to wonder why we hesitated to buy this magnificent horse the first time Mickey Denver asked."

"Me too," said Carole.

18

THE SUMMER DAY was a hot one, and by the time the sun was right overhead Carole and Lisa felt drained. Blondie had broken into a sweat, and even though she was going no faster than an ambling walk through the thick forest growth, there was lather all over her chest. But she kept going, doggedly obeying every request Lisa and Carole made.

As the narrow trail got steeper, Carole got off and walked, leading Blondie by her reins. When Lisa saw how profusely the horse was sweating, she knew she had to walk, too. She slid out of the saddle and walked in front of Carole and the horse.

"I'm not surprised the woman at the airport was concerned with how a rescue team might get to Phil and his uncle. This place is a jungle!" She swept a vine away from the path and held it aside while Blondie walked under it.

"And it looks to me as if it's going to get worse," Carole said.

"What?" Lisa asked. She was having trouble hearing Carole over a loud noise from above.

"I said—hey, look!" Carole said, pointing to the sky.

"Right, trees," Lisa said. Then she realized she had to say it very loudly. "No, not just trees," she corrected herself. "Airplane."

"More accurately, *rescue* airplane," said Carole.

It was, too. In the very few open spaces through the leaves, Lisa could see a small plane, white with a red cross on its fuselage, circling about half a mile ahead.

"They must see something!" Lisa said excitedly.

They both knew there was only one thing worth seeing from a rescue plane. They were near the wreckage. More important, they were near Phil and Uncle Michael.

"Come on. Let's hurry," said Lisa. "We've got to get to—"

She stopped because she didn't know what it was they had to get to. Both she and Carole were certain, from

Veronica's pictures and from the presence of the air-plane, that they were near where the glider had gone down, but they didn't know what they were going to find when they reached it. The unspoken question was why Phil and his uncle had failed to radio for help.

Lisa swallowed hard. This was no time to get scared. This was a time to follow the path blindly, just like Blondie. They would be the first to reach Phil and Uncle Michael. Their help would be the most important.

Seeking comfort as much as giving it, Carole patted Blondie on her sweat-streaked neck. "Come on, girl," she said. Blondie's nostrils flared. Her ears flicked attentively. Lisa and Carole were certain of one thing: Blondie wasn't giving up. Neither would they.

"Now let's go see how those two little girls are doing, Mrs. Hale," Moe said.

Deborah put down the pitchfork. She'd just mucked out two stalls. That should be enough to let Carole and Lisa get well out of sight.

"Okay," she agreed. "I bet my little Lisa is having the time of her life on that pony!"

Deborah followed Moe out the stable door. She followed him to the paddock fence. She followed him as he climbed up onto the fence.

"Where on earth could those little girls be?" he asked, confounded.

"Oh, I'm sure they're just having some fun with us," Deborah told him. "I'm not worried at all, and you shouldn't be, either."

"Okay," he said.

Deborah settled comfortably on the fence and shaded her eyes while she looked at the far end of the valley. She could see Rock Ridge. She could also see a small airplane circling the area. It had to be a rescue plane, and there was only one reason why it would keep circling. They'd spotted the wreckage!

"Moe, could I use the phone?" she asked.

PHIL SHADED HIS EYES and looked up to the sky where the airplane was circling above. He was standing on the tree branch right next to the glider, where his uncle Michael was now in considerable pain.

"They've spotted us, Uncle Michael," Phil said excitedly. "They know where we are. Help will come soon."

Uncle Michael smiled weakly and nodded.

Phil was glad he could give hope to Uncle Michael. His ankle was badly swollen. Phil had given him the one dose of morphine that he had. He didn't know how long it was going to last, and he didn't want to think about

159

how badly the ankle would hurt when it wore off. Another thing he didn't want to think about was how long it was going to take rescuers to reach them.

He knew how dense the forest was. The only open area for miles was Rock Ridge, and it had taken him over an hour to walk to it, less than a mile away. The fact that they'd been spotted *was* good news, but it wasn't the same as being rescued. It could take rescuers more than half a day to reach them.

Phil gave Uncle Michael a sip of water and then took one for himself. They shared a granola bar. It was the first thing Phil had had to eat since the night before. He hadn't known then how long their supplies would have to last.

"WHAT'S THAT?" Carole asked.

"I don't know," said Lisa. "It was a very strange sound."

"And it was coming from your pocket," Carole said.

Lisa patted her shirt pocket. There was the sound again.

"Oh, it's Deborah's cellular phone. I forgot she gave it to me to hold in the car. I wonder who's calling her?"

"So find out," Carole suggested logically.

It took two more rings for Lisa to figure out that the way to answer the phone was to push the SND button.

"Hello?"

"They've found them!"

"What?"

"Lisa, it's Deborah. I'm at the Denver ranch. I just talked to the woman at the airport. She tells me that the rescue plane found the wreckage. They couldn't see anybody because the trees are so thick, but they could see the glider. It's *in* a tree. Can you see the airplane overhead?"

Lisa looked up. The rescue plane was still circling ahead of them.

"Yes," Lisa said. "We figured it meant that was where they'd spotted the glider, so that's where we're headed."

"Keep the phone turned on so I can call you. I'll call you if there's any news, and if you need to reach me, all you have to do is press Redial and S-N-D because the last number I called using the cellular phone was the one I'm calling from now. Are you girls okay?"

"We're fine," Lisa assured her.

"And the horse?"

"A champion," Lisa said.

"Good," said Deborah. "Just like her riders."

"I'll call you when we get there," Lisa said.

They hung up.

Carole gave Blondie a well-deserved pat. "We're almost there, girl," she said. Blondie kept going.

Suddenly the trail turned sharply to the right, and they were completely out of the woods in bright sunlight.

"What's this?" Lisa asked, looking around her.

"This is Rock Ridge," said Carole. "More accurately, this is the *bottom* of Rock Ridge."

Lisa looked up to where the expanse of rock rose in front of her. "How the . . ."

"I think we climb," Carole said.

"Where?" Lisa glanced around, looking for a way they could get up to the top of the ridge.

"There," said Carole.

Lisa looked where her friend pointed. There was a very narrow set of steps, little more than footholds, chipped into the bedrock, that would carry nimble climbers up to the top of Rock Ridge. The girls looked at one another. It would be no trouble for them. But for a horse? This was why they had brought Blondie. Now they wondered, were they asking too much of her?

"Maybe there's another way," Carole said.

"Let's look then," said Lisa.

Carole fastened Blondie's reins to a branch. It went against her training to use reins to tie up a horse, but they hadn't brought a lead rope.

"Sorry, girl, but it's for your own good," Carole said.

Blondie didn't seem to mind. In fact, she seemed relieved to have a chance to rest. She sniffed out a bush
growing close to the ground and took a bite of it as if she
climbed mountains every day of her life and now it was
time for another ho-hum meal.

"We'll be back soon," said Lisa.

The girls scrambled up the steps to the top of Rock
Ridge. From there they had a view of the valley. It was
breathtaking, and if they hadn't been so hot, tired, and
worried, they might actually have enjoyed it.

While it seemed as if they could see the whole valley,
what they couldn't see was any way to avoid asking
Blondie to climb the slippery steps up the ridge to get
near where the airplane had been circling. To the east
and west the mountain fell away sharply.

Both girls were tired from walking and climbing. They
sat down to think.

"We could go back," Lisa said. "Then we'd come up
the other side of the mountain."

"And lose about four hours. We'd barely get there
before dark," said Carole.

Lisa scratched her head. If ever there was a time for
logical thinking, this was it. "We have to take the path
that will get us there the fastest without risking our lives
or the life of that brave horse. If we—Carole, what are
you looking at?"

163

Carole stood up and pointed across Rock Ridge. "Hey!" she said, and she started running. Lisa followed her.

"What is that?" Lisa asked, looking at a suitcase-sized bundle.

"It's a parachute," said Carole. Then they saw the remains of the little fire Phil had built.

"They're alive!" said Lisa, finally giving voice to the unspoken fear she and Carole had shared.

"Then why haven't they walked down to the valley?" asked Carole.

"They must need help," Lisa said.

The girls didn't talk anymore about what their choices were. There weren't any choices. They had to get to the glider. They had to do it fast, and they had to bring Blondie with them.

In a few minutes, they'd scrambled down the side of Rock Ridge and reached their willing horse. Lisa looked at the docile mare that had brought them so far.

"Do you really think . . . ?" she began.

"I really think that's why we've got a blind horse," Carole said. "We already know that this lady will do whatever we ask of her. She just doesn't know what it is we're going to ask, and I'm never going to tell her. We have to trust her inner vision. It's gotten us this far. I think it'll take us the rest of the way, too."

Lisa took the mare's reins and led her over to the steps on Rock Ridge. Blondie seemed to sense the urgency in Lisa's walk. She followed perfectly.

Lisa led from the left and Carole guided from the right. The trio paused at the bottom of the steep, narrow stone steps.

"Ready?" Lisa asked.

"Ready," Carole answered. She took Blondie's right foreleg and lifted it onto the first step.

Blondie obeyed patiently, step by step. She never moved backward; she never shied to the side. She had total faith in the humans who told her where to go and how to do it—almost as much faith as Lisa and Carole found they had in the horse.

It took more than forty-five minutes to make it up the steps to the top of Rock Ridge. Carole and Lisa both hugged the mare, whom they had come to love and admire more than they would have thought possible. Blondie lifted her head, turning it into the warm breeze that crossed the ridge. She sniffed eagerly, shook her head, and began walking forward. It was as if she understood there was no time to waste on silly signs of affection.

The far side of Rock Ridge was level with the forest. There was no climb down or up. The girls and Blondie simply walked into the woods.

165

"They can't be far now," Lisa said. "Otherwise we wouldn't have found that parachute."

"Well, let's see," said Carole. She cupped her hands around her mouth. "Phil!" she called. "Uncle Michael! Hello!"

There was no answer. They walked farther into the woods. Lisa spotted one of the blazes Phil had marked on a tree with the pocket knife. "It's a trail!" she said. "That's a fresh mark. They are definitely nearby."

Carole called out again. "Helloooooo! Phil! Uncle Michael! Can you hear me?"

They waited. There was only silence. They walked farther into the woods, looking for another blaze.

"Wait, do you hear something?" Lisa asked.

They stopped. It was quiet.

"Phil! Uncle Michael!" Carole repeated.

The girls waited. Blondie stood absolutely still.

There was a rustle in the woods ahead.

"Helloooo!" Carole called out.

They waited.

Ahead there was movement. Someone was coming.

"Phil?"

The boughs of two pine trees parted, and someone emerged from the dense woods, running toward the girls.

"Phil?" Lisa asked.

"Lisa? Carole?" he called out in stunned surprise.

"What are you doing here? With a *horse*? How did you get up here? How did you find us?"

"We've come to rescue you!" Lisa announced.

"I should have known The Saddle Club would come through!" said Phil, clearly near tears.

"We always do," Carole said calmly, giving him a hug. "Why didn't you use your radio?"

"It's a long story," said Phil.

"We've got time," Lisa said.

"Not as much as you think," Phil said ominously. "Come on!" He turned and hurried back the way he'd come. Carole and Lisa clucked their tongues and tugged gently at Blondie's reins. She followed them as they followed Phil.

Carole, Lisa, and Blondie scrambled through the thick forest to keep up with Phil. "It's this way," he called, following his own blazes between the crash site and Rock Ridge.

And then he stopped. The girls could see where he'd put some of his gear, a knife, matches, and a first aid kit, but there was no sign of the glider or Uncle Michael.

"Where's your uncle?" Carole asked.

"He's up there," said Phil, pointing. "He's got a broken ankle and can't climb down."

Carole and Lisa looked up. Stunned, Lisa put her hand over her mouth. Carole gasped. At once, they both remembered the words of Stevie's dream—*Phil is in a tree*.

"No, it couldn't be," said Lisa.

"Of course not," said Carole.

"I don't know what you girls are talking about, but Uncle Michael needs our help right now," said Phil.

Carole and Lisa looked back up the trunk of the tree. Whatever was going on with Stevie would have to wait.

19

PHIL STARTED CLIMBING the tree, and Lisa followed right after him. Carole patted Blondie and began to secure the mare's reins to a branch. This would be no time to have the mare wander off.

Then Carole had another thought. Maybe Blondie was going to be more helpful than she'd already been. She removed the lasso from the saddle horn of Blondie's Western saddle and slung the wreath of rope over one shoulder and under the other arm. It might just come in handy.

"Oh, wow, I wish I'd thought of that. It's perfect," Phil said as he watched Carole begin her ascent.

As soon as Carole reached the glider, she knew she'd been right.

Uncle Michael's face was a mask of pain, but he smiled weakly when he saw them all gathered around him.

"Is it visiting hours already?" he asked.

Phil and the girls laughed. Being able to joke was a good sign. When Carole showed him the rope, he suggested that it might be used to hang him. "I'm no use at all, you know," he said.

"You will be," Carole said, "as soon as we get you out of here."

"My ankle hurts so badly that I don't think I can move it at all, and I certainly can't climb down the tree."

"You won't have to do any climbing, I promise," Lisa said.

"Blondie will do all the work for you," Carole told him.

"You've got someone else with you?" asked Uncle Michael.

"In a manner of speaking," Lisa said. "Only it's not exactly a some*one*. It's more like a some*thing*." She began her explanation while Carole and Phil worked on the mechanics of the problem.

"Look, we can use the harness he's already wearing for his parachute," said Phil.

"Perfect," Carole agreed. She tossed one end of the rope over a large branch right above the pilot's seat and then slipped the end of rope through the parachute harness straps, securing it tightly with a knot.

"Where'd you learn to tie a knot like that?" Uncle Michael asked, clearly impressed.

"Oh, it's one of those Marine Corps things," Carole said. "Dad had to learn a bunch of knots when he was taking a survival course. He couldn't follow the instructions in the manual, so I figured them out and then taught him myself." Carole gave the rope a final tug, and, satisfied that it would hold, she began her descent to the ground.

She tied the rope to Blondie's saddle horn. On a signal from Phil, she got Blondie to move away from the tree.

Without ever discussing the matter, Carole, Phil, and Lisa each took a part of the task that they could do best. Carole was in charge of knots and Blondie. Phil took responsibility for guiding his uncle up and out of the glider and then down to the ground with the help of the rope and the parachute harness. Lisa knew that Phil's uncle was in a lot of pain, and she also knew that there wasn't anything she could do about it except to try to get him to concentrate on something else.

"Carole and I have a friend named Deborah," she began. "Deborah is an investigative reporter for a newspaper in Washington. You may have read some of her stories, like the time she discovered there was a scam going on in one of the federal departments. She does stories like that, but she also does more interesting things. Like a week ago, she heard a rumor that there was a horse trader not far from here . . ."

"Ouch!"

"Here you go, Uncle Michael. It's working!" As Blondie drew the rope tight, Phil helped guide his uncle out of the glider, where he'd been sitting for more than twenty-four hours.

". . . so Deborah needed a believable cover to be totally ignorant about horses . . ."

"You're out of there!" Phil said excitedly. He signaled Carole to stop Blondie while he helped Uncle Michael swing clear of the glider. Then he signaled her to walk back, slowly. "Okay, I'll climb down the tree to be sure you don't get tangled in any branches," Phil said, leading the way.

". . . and you wouldn't believe what this guy did," said Lisa.

Carole kept one eye on Blondie and another on Phil

and his uncle. Slowly, step by step, she and Blondie approached the tree and lowered Uncle Michael. Phil guided the man around the tree's lower branches, signaling Carole to pause from time to time. Carole wasn't sure what Lisa was doing, but whatever it was, Uncle Michael was paying attention to her and not to Phil and, best of all, not to his ankle.

"He thought you'd buy a horse without having a vet check it?" Uncle Michael asked. "You must have done a wonderful job playing an ignorant, fatuous, horse-loving girl!"

Lisa smiled proudly. "I guess I just have star quality," she said. "Anyway, both Carole and I knew something was really wrong with this horse . . ."

Suddenly there was slack in the rope and Uncle Michael wasn't moving. Phil looked up. The rope had gotten tangled in some small branches. He made Carole move back again to pull the rope taut, and he climbed back up the tree, leaving Uncle Michael dangling freely.

Uncle Michael looked up. A worried expression crossed his face.

"Well, what it was, of course, was that the horse was blind."

"How did you know?" asked Uncle Michael, letting Lisa's tale distract him again.

"The first hint was when the trader had to talk to her

173

constantly while she was walking over to him. The next was that he insisted on the lead rope . . ."

Phil tugged at the little branches, but they wouldn't budge. He shook his head to clear his mind. Someway, somehow. There had to be a way. "The knife, dummy," he said to himself. He patted his pocket and sighed with relief when he felt the bulk of the Swiss Army knife in his hip pocket. He flipped the large blade open, smiled to see the freshly honed blade glint in the sun, and started hacking off the small branches. With the right tool, it took only a second. The rope got a little frayed, but it held.

He nodded at Carole. "Slow, slow," Phil warned her.

Blondie stepped forward again. The rope moved over the branch. Uncle Michael moved down another foot. And then another, and another.

There was a groan. Phil, Carole, and Lisa all looked at Uncle Michael, but the groan hadn't come from him. It came from above him. It came from the glider.

It was the worst possible news. The glider, once securely tucked in the fork of the tree, was shifting its position because of the change in balance now that Uncle Michael was no longer in it. It loomed above them, perched precariously.

174

"I think we'd better move a little faster now," said Phil.

"Roger!" Carole agreed. She and Blondie began a steady pace, approaching the tree while Uncle Michael descended much faster than before.

"So, we just had to try this horse out again," said Lisa. "You know, part of it was curiosity about whether the horse trader would tell us . . ."

Another groan came from above. A branch snapped. Blondie sniffed. Her ears twitched anxiously.

"It's okay, girl," Carole assured her. They moved forward.

"We're almost there now, Uncle Michael," said Phil. He signaled Carole to bring Blondie right under the tree and Uncle Michael's feet.

Phil hopped off the last low branch of the tree. He and Carole adjusted the rope and the horse until Uncle Michael was lowered right into Blondie's saddle.

"You brought me up this mountain in your favorite form of transportation, Uncle Michael," Phil said. "Now, I get to take you down in mine!" He cut the rope.

Lisa jumped down from the lowest branch, glad to be on the ground, but not glad to be under the tree with the glider looming above. Another groan came from the plane.

"Let's move. Fast," she suggested. She didn't have to say it twice. Carole tugged at Blondie's reins, and Phil gave her a gentle, encouraging pat on her flanks.

They'd taken no more than three steps before the glider began tumbling down. Nobody looked back. They knew they were in danger. There was no way to predict what downward path the glider would take through the thick growth of the dense forest.

"Come on, Blondie!" Carole urged. The tired horse broke into a trot. Uncle Michael clutched the saddle horn. Carole, Lisa, and Phil ran alongside.

And then there was a final thunderous crash. The earth trembled under their feet. Dirt flew up around them. The air was filled with splinters, leaves, dust, and pine needles. Then there was silence.

All four of them stopped and turned around. The glider had slammed into the earth. The fuselage was cracked and smashed. It was hard for Phil to believe that only half an hour ago it had been sitting securely in the tree. What if it wasn't the jostling it got when they lifted Uncle Michael out that made it fall? What if it had fallen while Uncle Michael was still in it? The same thought flitted through Carole's and Lisa's minds.

"Don't think about that," said Uncle Michael, reading their minds. "We're all safe, and thanks to this wonderful horse you brought with you, I'm going to ride

176

down the mountain in style. Now, what did you say this fellow's name is?" he asked Carole.

"Blondie," Carole told him.

"What a coincidence," said Uncle Michael. "Isn't that the same name as the horse you were telling me about, the blind one?"

"Not just the same name," Lisa said. "It's the same horse."

"Are you telling me this horse is blind?" he asked, astonished.

"That's what I was trying to tell you the whole time you were coming down the tree. And you thought I had just made up a good story to distract you, didn't you?"

Uncle Michael swallowed hard. "Uh, Phil, I think you must have given me too big a dose of that pain medicine this morning. I think I'm hearing things and seeing things that can't be real."

"Don't worry, Uncle Michael," Phil assured him. "It's all very real. You just have a thing or two to learn about The Saddle Club. See, there's this bunch of riders who seem to think that any problem in the world can be solved with a horse—"

"Is that true?" Uncle Michael asked them.

"Of course it's true," Carole said. "And haven't we just proved it?"

An odd sound interrupted Carole's explanation. Carole and Phil looked at Lisa because it was coming from her pocket.

"Oh, the phone!" she said. She pulled it out of her pocket, flipped it open, and pressed SND. "Saddle Club Rescue Squad," she said, answering the phone.

As far as Lisa and Carole were concerned, the trip back down the mountain was a lot more pleasant than the one going up. They were no longer worried about Phil and his uncle. Deborah had promised she'd meet them in the valley, where an ambulance crew could take care of Uncle Michael's ankle.

The trip down was easier, too, because they didn't have to cross Rock Ridge. They took the long way down the other side of the mountain, knowing that the narrow steps that had been so hard to climb would be impossible for the blind horse to descend.

They couldn't wait to get Blondie to her paddock,

where she could have a long drink of water, a pile of fresh hay, and a well-deserved rest.

It was a long trip, it was hot, and it was difficult, yet Blondie never failed to do exactly what was asked of her.

"You girls are really something," said Uncle Michael.

"Well, we never could have done it without Stevie," said Lisa.

"What's she got to do with it?" Uncle Michael asked. "Hasn't she been laid up with a concussion?"

It wasn't an unreasonable question, but then, Uncle Michael didn't know Stevie.

"Boy, I want to see you explain this," said Phil, laughing at the situation.

"Here's the thing," Lisa began. "Stevie has a sort of special way of looking at things."

"Like nobody else," Carole added. "It's weird, but after a while, it starts rubbing off on you."

"Like, when you begin to think that maybe the best horse for the job is blind—now that's something only Stevie would think of," Lisa said.

"And when you figure out how to rig a lasso, intended for capturing dogies, to make it into an elevator—that's something Stevie would think of," said Phil.

"And when Carole figured out that the only way Moe would let us take Blondie out of the paddock was if

Deborah got him to teach her how to muck out a stall—that's pure Stevie," Lisa said.

"I think I'm beginning to get the idea," said Uncle Michael. "If it's absolutely wild and impossible, but it works, that's Stevie's way of doing it."

Phil and the girls laughed. "You are getting the idea," he told his uncle.

"Hey, look," said Lisa. "Is that a flashing light I see through the trees?"

Carole shaded her eyes and squinted. "Definitely," she said. "Red and white. It must be the ambulance."

"Then we're home free," said Phil.

"Phil, Carole, Lisa, I don't know how to thank you enough," said Uncle Michael. "You saved my life—and Stevie, too, I guess."

"Don't forget Blondie," Carole said.

"Never," Uncle Michael said, patting the old mare on her neck.

"Helloooo. Carole! Lisa! Is that you?" It was Deborah. They *were* safe, at last.

Blondie's ears perked up, and she picked up her pace. She practically trotted the last hundred yards through the now level forest to the open meadow in the valley.

It wasn't just an ambulance and Deborah that waited to greet them. There was a whole crowd. Max was there, along with a number of people from the Dunstable air-field. There were emergency personnel from the Rock Ridge fire department and emergency rescue service. The rescue service had started the treacherous climb up one side of the mountain and had been only too happy to abandon the dangerous trek when they got the word that the pilot and passenger had been rescued. The pilot from the rescue plane was there, and four reporters from local papers had come to get the story. Both of Lisa's parents had come, bringing Max with them, and so had Colonel Hanson. Phil's parents and his sisters were there, along with Uncle Michael's wife and their two children.

As soon as the group of rescuers emerged from the woods, the crowd began a round of applause that didn't stop until, it seemed to Lisa, everybody had hugged everybody else. It was a moment of triumph that they all enjoyed.

Then one more car pulled up next to the ambulance. Out of it came Mickey Denver. He stormed over to where Deborah was standing with Max and put his hands on his hips.

"What's this all about?" he demanded. "Moe told me that little girl of yours just rode out of the paddock without any permission from anyone. Now, what's it going to be? Are you going to buy Blondie or not?"

182

Deborah was stunned. So were Lisa and Carole and just about everybody else standing there. The only person who knew what to say was Phil.

"Of course we're going to buy her," he said.

And it was the right thing to say.

IT TOOK ABOUT an hour after that for everything to get sorted out. Carole and Lisa took Blondie back to her paddock and gave her a grooming, a big bucket of cool water, and a fresh flake of hay. Uncle Michael rode in the ambulance to the hospital with Phil's mother. Phil's father stayed behind to arrange for the purchase of Blondie—at a very favorable price. The rescue team made plans to climb back to the crash site so they could remove the remains of the glider in daylight and good weather.

Finally it was time to go. Carole, Lisa, and Phil all wanted to visit Stevie. Max and Deborah offered to drive them there since it was so close to Pine Hollow. Deborah said she was in a hurry to get home and start writing her article. Her undercover investigation had taken some very unexpected twists, and she could hardly wait to get to her computer.

The three young riders climbed into the backseat of Max's car. There was a lot to talk about. Number one, however, was Stevie.

183

"How did she know all those things?" Lisa asked, posing the question that had been on all of their minds. "It's amazing how she's been able to predict exactly what was going to happen or what had already happened and that she had no other way of knowing."

Phil shook his head. "I've been thinking about this a lot," he said.

"I bet you have," said Lisa. "You were there when she told you not to go in the glider. Remember when she said that an engine would be the problem?"

"Of course I remember, and the more I think about it, the less I believe it. Stevie hasn't been well. When people have head injuries, they can have pretty wild dreams. It's like the doctor said—her brain got rattled. That's all it is. It's the only possible explanation. Most of the time she doesn't even seem to remember what she dreamed about."

"And what about the sign for Veronica?" Carole asked. "She absolutely dreamed that."

"But that wasn't predicting the future," Phil said. "That was telling you what to do. And remember how I first thought she had a vision about what happened to me and Teddy? Well, I was being silly. Like you said, it was almost exactly the same thing that had happened to her. She was reliving her own nightmare."

184

"Okay," Lisa conceded. "Some things really aren't at all significant. But a few were pretty eerie. I mean, remember that she knew Blondie was blind even before we told her?"

"You both knew it, though, and you may have told her in some way you didn't even know. I mean, like body language."

"Possibly," Carole said. "But how about the way she knew you were in a tree?"

"It's not hard to understand that one," said Phil. "At first, Stevie was upset I was going gliding because it was going to interfere with our jump competition. So when she couldn't go ahead with the jump competition, she got more upset and became worried that something would happen to me. She knew we'd be flying over woods. The fact that her nightmare included Uncle Michael's glider being *in* a tree was pure coincidence."

Max joined the conversation as he drove. "See, girls, there's a logical explanation for everything. It all starts because you're concerned about Stevie. That's natural enough. But there is no such thing as being able to read other people's minds or being able to tell the future."

"Oh, I don't know about that," said Deborah.

"What do you mean?" Max asked.

"Well, remember when Stevie called me Mom?"

185

"I do," said Lisa. "I promise you, neither Carole nor I had had a chance to tell her about how much fun it was to call you Mom, but she seemed to know it anyway."

"Right. We hadn't even mentioned it, so there's no way she could have known," Carole said.

"Oh, that wasn't exactly what I meant," said Deborah. "Maybe that's what it was, though."

Max turned and looked at her. "Do you think you should tell this group that there is something else she might have foreseen?" he asked, his voice dripping with irony.

Deborah grinned. "Could be," she said.

"A new little rider is coming to Pine Hollow?" Carole asked.

"Max the Fourth?" Lisa asked.

"Could be," said Deborah. "Could be."

"Wow!" said Lisa, hugging Deborah excitedly but carefully.

"Yahooo!" Carole declared, patting Max on the back so vigorously that the car swerved.

"I wonder if Stevie knows that already!" said Phil.

Everybody laughed, and then cheered.

STEVIE HAD NO IDEA about Max and Deborah's baby. But she said she thought it was going to be a nice thing for them.

That wasn't the reaction her friends had expected. They'd thought she'd be as excited as they were. Stevie didn't seem to be in a mood to get excited about much of anything.

"Now let me get this straight," Stevie said, shifting in her bed. She was staring intently at Lisa, Carole, and Phil. "You two took a blind horse up onto a mountain to rescue Phil because that's what I would have done?"

187

Lisa and Carole nodded. "That's right," Lisa said. "You would have been so proud of us!"

"I would have had your heads examined," Stevie said.

"We never would have thought of doing it if it hadn't been for the dream you had. That, combined with the photographs that Veronica showed us, told us exactly what had happened, and there really was only one thing to do once we had the information," Carole told her.

Lisa nodded agreement. "And the woman at the airport told us that there really was no way any kind of rescue vehicle ever could have gotten to where the glider was," she said. "The horse was perfect."

"But a horse that wasn't blind probably wouldn't have made it, either. No sighted horse with any common sense would have been willing to climb Rock Ridge," Carole said.

"So even though you were here in bed, both of us felt as if you were with us every step of the way—you and your dreams, I mean."

Stevie shook her head. "There you go, talking about my dreams again. What on earth do a couple of strange dreams have to do with anything? They're just dreams."

"Right, like Belle is just a horse," said Carole.

"Belle isn't just a horse," Stevie corrected her quickly. "But at least we all know that Belle is real. I don't even remember having the kinds of dreams you keep telling me I had."

"You don't remember saying Phil was in a tree?" Lisa asked.

"Nope," Stevie said positively.

"What about when you told us that Blondie had vision even though she was blind?" Carole asked. "That sure turned out to be true. It was as if she had some kind of sixth sense that calmed and guided her every step of the way."

"How can a blind horse have vision?" Stevie asked. "That's just not logical."

Logic was not something that Stevie had ever much concerned herself with before. It was this kind of thinking that made her friends worry about her. Was the real Stevie ever going to come back? Would this be a permanent change?

Phil, Carole, and Lisa all glanced at one another. Lisa shrugged ever so slightly. The doctor kept insisting that Stevie was getting better. Could he be right?

"Well, with or without your help, a few things have gone right," said Carole. "Number one is that when Uncle Michael and I reported the behavior of the pilot of Mr. diAngelo's plane, his license got suspended for a good long time."

"Yes!" Lisa declared.

"And number two is that Veronica is not going to win the photographic contest," said Carole. "At least not with pictures of a glider that's about to crash."

"Really?" Phil asked. "How do you know that?"

"Well, it seems that the rules of the contest require that the photographs be taken without any adult help. Hubert, childish as he is, is an adult, and by flying the plane, he was helping Veronica. Those photographs are all disqualified!"

"Oh no!" said Lisa.

"What's wrong with that?" Carole asked.

"It means she won't be gone for two weeks!" Lisa said.

"Oh, don't be so sure of that," said Carole. "When last seen, she was storming around saying she didn't care a whit for that dumb old picture contest and she was going to get her daddy to let her go to Rome. She'd have a much nicer time going with her mummy, anyway. After all, her mummy is the one with all the credit cards!"

"Do you think we should warn the Italians about the invasion?" Lisa asked.

Phil laughed. "No, they'll figure it out. And besides, they'll only have to put up with her for two weeks. We'll have her for the other fifty weeks of the year!"

"And then there's number three," Carole said. "And that's Blondie. Phil's father bought her from Mickey

Denver. Uncle Michael said a horse that wonderful needed to have a wonderful retirement, so now she's living in a field next to Phil's house."

"Where she'll get a well-deserved rest and lots of love. And an occasional trail ride," said Lisa.

"But no mountains, no rocky ridges, and no more rescue missions," Carole said.

"Definitely," said Phil.

Stevie fluffed her pillow irritably. "This is all very interesting, I'm sure, but can you carry on about it someplace else? I've got some reading to do from my summer reading list."

"Stevie, school just let out," Lisa said. "You don't have to read those books for two months!" She herself had begun work on her summer reading list the day after school closed, but it was more Stevie's style to begin the work the day before school opened than two months ahead of time.

"Just two months?" Stevie said. "Well, there isn't a moment to waste. Has anyone seen my copy of *Silas Marner?*"

"You're reading *Silas Marner?*" Phil asked, surprised.

"*Moby Dick* was out of the library when Chad went over there for me," Stevie explained.

"You wanted to read *Moby Dick?*" Carole asked, stunned.

"Until I can find my copy of *War and Peace*," Stevie said, as if that explained anything. "Oh, there it is," she said, spotting her book on the other side of the room. She sat up straight in bed and shifted her legs so that she could stand up.

"Here, Stevie, I'll give you a hand," Phil said.

"No, I'm okay," Stevie insisted. "I didn't break anything. I can walk all right."

She stood up. Her friends knew that she'd barely been out of bed for almost a week, and that was enough to make anybody unsteady as they walked. Stevie was adamant, though. She was tired of being confused by the odd things that people said and the odd way they were treating her. She wanted to show them that she could walk across her bedroom, pick up a book, and walk back. She held the footboard of her bed for a moment to steady herself. Then, when she thought she was ready, she took a step, and then another one.

That was when the most peculiar thing began to happen. For some reason, the room began to spin. At first it moved slowly. Then it was a total sea of confusion. Lisa, Carole, and Phil seemed to spin with the room. Stars appeared in midair, their bright glare washing everything away from Stevie's sight.

"Stevie?" Lisa asked.

"Are you all right?" asked Carole.

"Let me help you," said Phil.

"I'm fine," said Stevie. "I've never felt better in my life."

And then the whole world was a blank.

"Catch her! She's falling!" Lisa screamed.

Phil, Carole, and Lisa all ran to catch Stevie, but they were too late. Stevie's legs simply collapsed, and she hit the floor with a bang. More accurately, her head hit the floor with a bang, and she was completely unconscious.

"Oh no! Not again!" Lisa cried.

The three of them gathered around Stevie. Lisa picked up her wrist and felt for a pulse. It was there. Carole noted that she was breathing evenly. Phil held her hand.

They waited a minute.

Stevie's eyes fluttered open. She blinked a few times. She reached up to her head and rubbed the bump that was swelling up.

"Ouch!" she declared. Then, while her friends watched, wondering what would happen, Stevie pulled herself to a sitting position.

A fiery look of anger came over her face. She took a deep breath and spoke. "Where is that Veronica di-Angelo?" she demanded. "I want to give that girl a piece of my mind. Can you believe she took a flash picture right in our faces so that Belle got spooked and I hit my head?"

"It's Stevie!" Lisa said, thrilled.

"She's back!" said Carole. They both knew their friend when they saw her. This was the real Stevie, the one who loved to laugh, play practical jokes, get into trouble, and eat butter pecan ice cream with licorice bits.

"What am I doing out of bed now?" Stevie asked, still apparently confused.

"You were getting your copy of *Silas Marner,*" Phil explained, smiling.

"Why would I be doing that?" Stevie asked. "School doesn't start for at least two months! Man, I'm starving. Do you suppose there's anything to eat in the house? I could really go for some key lime sherbet with caramel sauce and mint sprinkles."

Lisa and Carole looked at one another and then slapped their hands together in a high five. The Saddle Club was together again!

ABOUT THE AUTHOR

BONNIE BRYANT is the author of many books for young readers, including novelizations of movie hits such as *Teenage Mutant Ninja Turtles* and *Honey, I Blew Up the Kid*, written under her married name, B. B. Hiller.

Ms. Bryant began writing The Saddle Club in 1986. Although she had done some riding before that, she intensified her studies then and found herself learning right along with her characters Stevie, Carole, and Lisa. She claims that they are all much better riders than she is.

Ms. Bryant was born and raised in New York City. She still lives there, in Greenwich Village, with her two sons.

Don't miss Bonnie Bryant's next exciting Saddle Club
adventure . . .

TIGHT REIN
The Saddle Club #57

Stevie Lake has been grounded. No hanging out with
the other members of The Saddle Club. Even worse,
Stevie's not allowed to see her horse, Belle, or go to
riding camp. Carole and Lisa have to get their friend
out of hot water—and back in the saddle. But without
Stevie around, how are they going to devise the kind
of wacky plan it will take to spring her *and* get sweet
revenge on her brother, Chad, who got Stevie in trouble in the first place? Carole and Lisa have to do
something rash. If they don't, summer is going to be a
complete bust!

Read all The Saddle Club Super Editions by
Bonnie Bryant! Each one is packed full of
extra action. . . .

#1 A SUMMER WITHOUT HORSES

When Stevie can't ride for a while, Lisa and Carole
make a pact not to ride until their friend has recov-
ered. After all, they're The Saddle Club, and they
always stick together. To seal the pact, the girls decide
that if any of them breaks the vow, they'll have to ask
stuck-up Veronica diAngelo to join their club. That'll
keep them out of the saddle for sure!

But can three horse-crazy girls really stay away from
horses and riding for more than a day? Find out in this
super edition, which contains three separate stories
about Lisa, Stevie, and Carole—and their summer
without horses.

#2 THE SECRET OF THE STALLION

It's going to be the most amazing Saddle Club adventure ever! The girls are traveling to horsey old England. They'll ride in a show on the grounds of a real castle. Lisa has done some homework and discovered an ancient unsolved mystery about the duke who once lived there. The duke buried treasure under the stall of his spirited stallion. Then tragedy struck—the barn burned down, and the stallion perished. A year later the duke's body was found on the same spot, his hand clutching a single fire opal. . . . Legend says the treasure will be found by a rider with fire in his heart.

The girls are busy with the show, sight-seeing in London, and getting ready for a costume ball at the castle. On that night, it seems that almost anything could happen—but the story of the duke, his stallion, and the tragedy of the burning barn couldn't replay itself, could it?

#3 WESTERN STAR

The girls can't wait for winter break from school. Carole, Stevie, and Lisa are heading West to spend the first part of their vacation at one of their favorite places—the Bar None Ranch.

But what they thought would be a quick trip turns into a snowbound adventure. The girls must rescue a herd of horses that face a terrible fate. . . .

Join The Saddle Club on an unforgettable journey that recalls the true spirit of giving and the strength of friendship.

Saddle Up For Fun!
Join The Saddle Club

As an official Saddle Club member you'll get:

- *Saddle Club newsletter*
- *Saddle Club membership card*
- *Saddle Club bookmark*
- *and exciting updates on everything that's happening with your favorite series.*

Bantam Doubleday Dell Books for Young Readers
Saddle Club Membership Box BK
1540 Broadway
New York, NY 10036

SKYLARK

Bantam Doubleday Dell
Books for Young Readers

Name _____

Address _____

City _____ **State** _____ **Zip** _____

Date of birth _____

Offer good while supplies last.

BFYR - 8/93